FK
7.00

I am aware, sir," Jocelyn said slowly, "of the marriage contract my brother signed. The agreement was that I marry you, which I have done. There was nothing in the contract that stated I had to live with you. Now that I have fulfilled my part of the agreement, I consider myself free to leave."

Sir Rolf began to laugh. "Apparently you do not know as much as you think about your brother's bargain. The day you leave me is the day the money stops. And I do not imagine that your money-hungry brother is going to let you go home, probably not even for a short visit."

Jocelyn stared at the floor, all hope gone.

"You are my wife, and nothing can change that," Sir Rolf said. "So you would do well to act accordingly."

She looked up at the triumphant expression on his face and knew she despised him, *just as she knew she was trapped for life in a marriage she hated.*

A
Strange and Ill-Starred
Marriage

A NOVEL BY

Helen Tucker

A FAWCETT CREST BOOK • NEW YORK

A STRANGE AND ILL-STARRED MARRIAGE

Published by Fawcett Crest Books, CBS Publications, the Consumer Publishing Division of CBS Inc.

ISBN: 0-449-23535-1

Printed in the United States of America

10   9   8   7   6   5   4   3   2   1

A
Strange and Ill-Starred
Marriage

One

A sudden iciness, which had nothing to do with the roaring fire in the hearth, swept through the room. Jocelyn, who had been standing beside her brother's chair looking down at Gerard as though every word he uttered were in jest, went quickly to hearthside to warm herself as a chill all but overcame her. Only now did she realize that Gerard had not been making a poor joke at her expense; he was deadly serious.

She stared down at the fire, her mind refusing to take hold of the words Gerard had said. Her hair, dark as a raven's wing, fell across her forehead as she rubbed her hand over her head, and her face, which usually wore an expression of extreme serenity, had little worry-furrows around her mouth and near her blue-gray eyes.

Finally she turned and faced Gerard again, glaring; and he glared back at her, his expression saying clearly, "You had better listen more closely and believe me, little sister, for I am telling you about your future."

Well, she thought, what could he say now that would be any worse than what he had said to her already? He had offered her, his only sister, in marriage to Sir Rolf Caradoc, known throughout the countryside as an unconscionable scoundrel.

"No, no, my dear Jocelyn, you have it all wrong,"

7

Gerard was saying when she forced herself to listen to him again. "Sir Rolf has offered for *you*."

"He has offered for every girl of decent family in Buckinghamshire and, I have heard, even in London; and the reason he has reached his great age without a wife is because no father with even a modicum of self-respect would allow his daughter to marry that vile . . ."

"He is only forty-two," Gerard interrupted. "Not such a great age."

"More than twice my age," Jocelyn retorted hotly. She still could not quite take it in that Gerard had done this terrible thing, but if true—as it would seem to be—she was confident that she could reason with him, make him see what a dreadful mistake he had made.

He was looking at her now in a patronizing way, as though she were wanting in sense, or possibly merely acting childish. His face, unlike the expressive face of Jocelyn, was unreadable. The Egmont brother and sister were as far apart in their ways as they were in appearance. Where Jocelyn was thoughtful and deliberate in actions, Gerard was impulsive, sometimes rash; where Jocelyn was slow to anger (but once angered, even slower to recover), Gerard had a quick temper that raged like a brief summer storm and then died down. In appearance, Gerard's light brown hair and somewhat coarse features contrasted totally with Jocelyn's dark, delicate beauty.

"Gerard, I believe you must have gone mad," she said finally. "Completely mad."

Gerard ignored her remark and said, "Your twentieth birthday will be in a fortnight. We shall celebrate your wedding the same day." Then, looking into her distraught face, he added, "Come, Jocelyn, be happy. Think of the future you will have as mistress of Caradoc Court. Sir Rolf is known to be the wealthiest man in this part . . ."

"He is known to have had his way with every tavern

wench to come into his view, and his bad nature is as well known as his odious reputation with women. God is witness to the fact, Gerard, that I would not marry that man if my life depended upon it."

"Your life *does* depend upon it." Gerard gave her a hard, cold look. "And mine as well."

Jocelyn gave a little gasp. She knew only too well what he was saying, or rather, what he was *not* saying. He was telling her that he had gone through their inheritance in the two years since their father's death and there probably was little left. Gerard's frequent trips to London and the continent, his hours spent in the gaming houses, were well known to her.

"You will simply have to learn to be more provident, Gerard," she said. "I will not let you sacrifice me to your extravagances."

He crossed the room in three steps and grasped her arm, his fingers biting into her flesh even through the thickness of the sleeve. "It is no longer a matter of extravagance; it is a matter of survival. There is nothing left, nothing; and our debts . . ."

"Your debts!"

"Yours also, and there is no way to pay them. We will lose this house, everything, unless you marry Sir Rolf."

"Then we shall lose everything," she said, "because I shall never marry that viper."

"I signed an agreement yesterday at Caradoc Court," Gerard said. "Sir Rolf is most eager to take a bride so that he may have an heir to whom he can leave his vast estate. Without an heir, it will all go to his brother, Edward, and it seems that Sir Rolf cannot abide his brother. Just the thought of Edward's being the master of Caradoc Court puts his lordship into a towering temper."

Jocelyn heard nothing save the words that an agreement had been signed. "You have sold me!" she said in a harsh whisper. "For how many pieces of silver did you sell me, my good and kind brother?"

"Do not be sarcastic with me, Jocelyn. I had no choice. Married to Sir Rolf, you will have everything. Not married to him, we shall both lose everything, including these walls which now shelter us from that cold April rain outside."

Jocelyn looked forlornly at the window, absent-mindedly watching the raindrops run together and slide down the glass. They reminded her of teardrops, but she could not afford to cry now, for crying was a form of surrender and she still had to wage battle with Gerard.

"I am sorry you signed a marriage agreement for me, for that is one agreement you will never be able to keep," she said. "If you continue to insist on this insanity, I shall leave home—run away, if necessary."

"And where, pray, would you run? There is nowhere for you to go without money. There are no relatives to take you in."

She stared down at the stone hearth again, recognizing the truth of his words. There was nothing she could do but stay and submit to the indignities of marriage to Sir Rolf Caradoc, whom she could remember having seen only once or twice, but about whom she had heard nothing but evil. "Gerard," she said, thinking to make one last attempt to save herself, "remember, you promised me quite some time ago that you would take me with you to London for the High Season, and I could find a suitable husband there. I have been looking forward to that for a long time."

"It is too late for that," he said. "The cost of spending the Season in London is dear indeed. Besides, I have found a suitable husband for you right here in the county."

He looked at her and briefly touched her shoulder, then went back to his chair. For a moment, she thought he would have compassion for her when he said, "I am sorry, Jocelyn. I am truly sorry." But then he added, "You must realize that these plans for you are not only necessary, but also in the long run will be to your advantage," and she knew that there was no way he could be made to change his mind, that there was no hope for her now.

The fact was, there had been no hope for her since yesterday when Gerard had sat with Sir Rolf in the great hall at Caradoc Court sipping a brandy after signing the paper prepared by Sir Rolf's barrister, and pocketing the check signed by Sir Rolf.

Jocelyn could feel the tears coming to surface and knew that she was going to begin to cry in earnest. She started from the room.

"Wait," Gerard said. "I trust you were merely making empty threats when you said you would run away. I am sure you realize the futility of that. But I want your word that you will not try, for it could prove embarrassing to Sir Rolf if it became known about the countryside that you were an unwilling bride."

"I will give you my word on nothing," she responded.

"Then it will be necessary to keep you under lock and key until the wedding."

Would he do that, keep her locked in her room like a recalcitrant child? She looked at him closely and decided that he would.

"All right," she said. "You have my word. Now may I ask why you are in such unseemly haste for this marriage?"

"The reason should be obvious," Gerard said. "I can do nothing with the check Sir Rolf gave me until after the ceremony. And also, both he and I thought your birthday anniversary would make a perfect wedding day."

She could listen to no more. She fled from the room to her bedroom upstairs and flung herself into the arms of her abigail, Irva, sobbing as though it were the last day of the world.

Jocelyn cried until there were no tears left and all the while Irva stroked her back, saying over and over, "What is it, Miss Jocelyn? Oh, miss, whatever is the matter?" But Jocelyn, when she finally stopped crying, had neither the breath nor the inclination to talk—not even to Irva, who was only a few years her senior and who had served for years as something of a confidante as well as abigail.

She went to her bed and fell across it, staring moodily at the ceiling as she nursed a sudden and uncontrollable hatred for her brother. It was inconceivable that Gerard could have done such a terrible thing to her; and yet, the more she thought about it, the more in character it seemed, for Gerard had changed greatly for the worse since the death of their father two years before. Something of a father's boy from the time he was about ten, Gerard had followed Harold Egmont about the estate like a second shadow. Jocelyn, four years younger than Gerard, could count among her earliest memories the sight of her brother sitting behind their father on the big roan stallion, Gerard's little arms tightly encircling his father's waist. The bond between father and son became even closer after the death of their mother when Gerard was sixteen and Jocelyn twelve. It was then that Irva, mature at fifteen, became Jocelyn's abigail and helped her young mistress in the running of the household.

Harold Egmont died of pneumonia contracted on a fox hunt in the early spring exactly four years after the same malady had felled his wife. Gerard, inconsolable, had for months withdrawn inside himself, taking no interest in house or land, friend or family.

Jocelyn did what she could, but there seemed to be no way to bring her brother out of his despondency. However, several months after their father's death, Gerard found it necessary to go to London to consult a barrister about the estate. It was his first trip to the city and, apparently, he fell in with bad company. Away for nearly a fortnight, he was a changed person when he returned. Although he still seemed a bit withdrawn, he was no longer despondent and he began to go to parties and balls in the nearby village and, after that, he began to make frequent trips to London and then to the continent.

It was only six months ago that Jocelyn had found out that Gerard was spending most of his time and, as it turned out, all of their money in gaming houses. While Gerard was away on one of his trips abroad, a letter arrived from the London barrister. Thinking it might be urgent business, Jocelyn opened the letter. It was a warning to Gerard that the modest inheritance left to him and his sister was dwindling and that it behooved him to handle his affairs better in the managing of his money. It also contained a stern warning about the foolhardiness of squandering the inheritance in gaming houses and ended by saying, "It is likely that you shall, if you continue in this vein, end your days in a debtors' gaol."

Jocelyn had read that sentence over several times, unable to comprehend how Gerard could be foolish enough to allow their finances to reach such a point. He would simply have to stay home and take care of their land and stop squandering what was left of their meager funds.

But Gerard had taken care of the situation in another way—by offering his sister to the wealthiest man in the county—for a price. A great price, no doubt, Jocelyn thought wryly. Probably Gerard would never have to worry about money again; he could enjoy himself in gaming houses all over the world now.

She sat up and looked around her bedroom as though for the last time—and, indeed, it soon would be. The thought of leaving Egmont House made her want to start crying again, but she refrained. She had loved her home since she was old enough to understand a feeling for a place. The house was furnished with heirlooms from many generations (strange, almost miraculous, that Gerard had not thought of selling them); and the gardens outside with their many kinds of roses were the result of her father's labor of love, for though they had a gardener, Harold Egmont, whose greatest enjoyment was in seeing how many varieties of rose he could make bloom, had tended the gardens faithfully.

The house itself, set back from a seldom traveled road in a grove of beeches and oaks, had a look of simple elegance. Built during the latter part of the Tudor reign, it contained all the best in architecture of that period. It had been in the Egmont family from the beginning.

And Jocelyn was to give up all of this for Caradoc Court, a place she had never seen, a place she was sure she could never like, let alone love as she loved this house.

It came to her suddenly—the one time she distinctly remembered seeing Sir Rolf, her husband-to-be. It was shortly before the death of her father and Sir Rolf had come to call on him. The two men were sitting together talking in the garden late one afternoon when Jocelyn went to see whether the visitor would remain overnight. As she approached, she heard her father say in angry tones, "Sir, you do us no honor, and I will not hear of such a thing!"

Fearing to disturb an argument, she drew back into the hedges to wait for a lull in the conversation.

"She is much too young, and I mean to keep her here with me for a long time yet," her father continued.

"Then you do her no favor," the visitor said. "You are depriving her of a more abundant life and . . ."

"I warn you, I want to hear no more about it, sir. You have dishonored your name, and I feel that your presence here dishonors mine. I should appreciate it if you left immediately!"

"You are a stubborn man, Harold Egmont, and I wager the day will come when you will rue your haughtiness."

Jocelyn had never seen her father so agitated. He passed by the hedgerow near enough for her to touch on his way into the house. The visitor stood for a minute or two by the stone bench watching his departing host, then he too left the garden. Sir Rolf was a large man, big-boned as well as slightly obese. His brown hair receded from his high forehead, and his eyes, always small, seemed narrowed to slits as he stared at the back of Harold Egmont. His mouth, open a little, had a slack look.

Jocelyn stayed in the hedgerow until Sir Rolf mounted his horse and rode away. She assumed that the conversation had been about a servant girl whom the visitor probably wanted to take for his own household staff.

Now, however, she surmised that she herself had been the subject, that Sir Rolf had offered for her that afternoon, and that her father had sent the man away, enraged that the scoundrel would even consider offering for his daughter.

It was only a short time later that Jocelyn began to hear talk in the village, indeed, throughout the county, about Sir Rolf, his reputation, and the fact that he was going everywhere trying to find a well-born wife to be mistress of Caradoc Court and to give him an heir.

"He's probably got heirs a-plenty all over the countryside," Jocelyn overheard one of the Egmont servants say, "but not one that he can claim. I wager he's populated all of Buckinghamshire with his bastards."

And this was the man to whom Gerard had promised her! Gerard was an unmitigated beast, with no more thought for the feelings and well-being of his sister than a vicious animal would have.

"I cannot go through with it."

She was not aware that she had spoken aloud until Irva remarked, "What can you not go through with, miss?"

Jocelyn looked at her abigail, wondering suddenly what arrangements, if any, Gerard had made for Irva. Was she to accompany her mistress to Caradoc Court, or would she remain here as one of the household staff?

"Sir Rolf Caradoc has offered for me in marriage and my brother has accepted," she said, in such a low tone of voice that her abigail had to strain to hear.

"Oh, miss, no! This cannot be true!" The shock in Irva's face and voice told Jocelyn that Sir Rolf's reputation was as well known to her abigail as it was to herself.

"It is true," she said as the tears began anew.

"Not Sir Rolf! I am certain Mr. Gerard would not permit you to marry him, let alone accept for you." But even as she said it, Irva knew that it was true, for she had never known her mistress to behave in this manner before. "We will pack a bag and go away from here. If he does not know where you are, Mr. Gerard cannot force you to marry."

Jocelyn gave a bitter laugh. "Gerard has already shown me the folly of trying to leave. He pointed out, and rightly, that there is nowhere for me to go. Besides, with no money, we could not get very far."

Money. She thought again of the bargain Gerard had struck. Probably Sir Rolf had promised her brother a lifetime income. Had not Gerard said, "Your life depends upon it—and mine as well."

"Sir Rolf has a good name," Irva said, "but one which he has ill served, I think."

"True, and it has been a number of years since any decent people would associate with him," replied Jocelyn, remembering how her father had ordered the man to leave. "Certainly none would consider him as a husband for a daughter or sister. Only Gerard."

She spoke her brother's name with such bitterness that it sent a shiver through Irva. Though brother and sister had never been particularly close, they had always treated each other with civility, even a certain deference, and it was hard for Irva to imagine any circumstances under which Mr. Gerard would accept Sir Rolf Caradoc as a husband for his sister. Though born a gentleman, Sir Rolf most assuredly had not lived as one. His scandalous behavior had been the talk of the countryside for as long as Irva could remember, and it was obvious from the distress of her mistress that at least some of the talk had reached her ears also.

"There must be some way the marriage can be prevented," Irva said finally.

"If there is, I shall think of it," Jocelyn said, her usually buoyant spirit returning. "I shall devote the next two weeks to nothing but thinking of a way to prevent the wedding." Already her mind was at work. She could feign illness, beginning with fainting spells . . .

But, her good judgment told her, it would take only one visit from the doctor to reassure Gerard of his sister's good health. And if she had any complaints of health at all, they would only serve as a possible way of delaying the ceremony. Eventually the marriage would take place; Gerard would see to that.

"Has a date been named?" Irva asked.

"In a fortnight. On my twentieth birthday anniversary."

"Oh, surely not, miss!"

There was a knock at the door, and without waiting for answer, Gerard entered. "Leave us, please, Irva," he said. "I wish to speak to my sister alone."

With a dark glance toward Gerard, Irva went out.

"I was not aware that we had anything further to say to each other," Jocelyn said, "unless you, perhaps, have changed your mind about making me go through with this travesty of a marriage."

"There will be no change, either of mind or plan," Gerard said. "I came in here hoping to find a change of attitude on your part now that you have had more time to get used to the idea. Come, Jocelyn, is it so bad that I want to assure you of a good future?"

"Had you not been such a wastrel these past two years, my good future would have been assured," she retorted.

"Now, Jocelyn . . ."

"You are no better than the scoundrel to whom you would marry me."

Gerard drew back and looked at her coldly. "I cannot understand why you continue to believe the worst of my action in your behalf. If you would use your reason, my dear sister, you would know that I have acted in your best interests." He went to the door, opened it, then turned to her again. "Regardless of what you believe or what you feel, the marriage will take place."

He went out and closed the door before she could answer. She picked up the thick porcelain bowl from the marble top of the washstand and, in her frustration, threw it with all her might against the door. The bowl fell to the thick carpet without breaking, and this struck Jocelyn as being symbolic of the marriage agreement Gerard had signed at Caradoc Court. It, too, would remain unbroken, no matter how she raged against it.

She fell back against the pillows of her bed once more, feeling the onslaught of another storm of tears.

Grotesque was the word used most often by those who endeavored to describe Caradoc Court. Originally named Fenwick Manor by the builder, Sir Rolf's great-great-grandfather, the house was enlarged and completely changed by Sir Rolf himself in the past ten years, and it was he who named the result of ·the changes Caradoc Court. The house was enormous to begin with, as befitted the domicile of the largest landowner in the county, and it was a rather handsome graystone dwelling, but when it became increasingly obvious to Sir Rolf that it was going to be difficult for him to find a bride from the Polite World, he decided an even larger, more ostentatious house would serve as an enticement not only for the prospective bride, but also her family whose objections had to be overcome before he could pay court to any girl.

His knowledge of architecture was limited to the point of being almost nonexistent, yet he desired to do the designing himself. The result was a rectangular house, with part of the fourth side left open as an entryway into the courtyard. Bedrooms, each with a small dressing and sitting room, were in one side of the house; the great hall, a smaller dining room, and a ballroom were in another; and the quarters of the household staff were in the third side, along with a small room where Edward Caradoc kept accounts for the estate and did his paperwork. The abbreviated side of the rectangle contained an afterthought of Sir Rolf's which he deemed the epitome of cleverness —a chapel. Surely, he reasoned, having the chapel and calling frequently upon the services of the vicar from the village would be of great help in healing his badly wounded reputation as well as in re-establishing himself in the Polite World. However, the chapel, like the ball-room, had never been used, for what Sir Rolf had not taken into consideration was the fact that his years of dalliance with tavern wenches and maidservants, his years of playing the rogue, had rendered the wound to his reputation mortal. Families not only would not listen to his offers for their daughters, but would not even enter-tain him in their homes.

The stonemasons did what they could with Sir Rolf's elaborate designs—which included gargoyles in every corner and along the ceilings of almost every room— but they shook their heads sadly as they went about their work, as though they were being forced under pain of death to commit a sacrilege.

It took quite some time after the completion of Caradoc Court for Sir Rolf to realize that all the changes were in vain, including the attempted reform of his own character, and that he might as well go back to taking his pleasure where he could, for he was not going to find a proper young woman who would marry him and give him an heir.

That was the way the situation had stood until six weeks ago when Gerard Egmont had paid him a surprise visit. Sir Rolf had been in the courtyard inspecting some new horseflesh when Gerard rode up, dismounted, and gave the reins to a servant.

"Good-day to you, sir," he said, recognizing Caradoc

before he himself was recognized.

"And to you," Sir Rolf said, realizing that this was the son of the late Harold Egmont. "What brings you to Caradoc Court? As I remember, the Egmont house is a good distance from here, so I gather you are not just out for a ride."

"I have business with you, sir," Gerard said, believing it better to come straight to the point.

"Then let us go inside," Sir Rolf said, leading the way to the small dining room. "I was about to have my tea," he said to his unexpected visitor. "May I offer you some, or perhaps wine or a brandy would be more to your liking."

Sir Rolf smiled as he said it. He seldom drank tea himself and had been testing his guest as well as playing a game with himself, trying to see if he could guess the nature of the business by what young Egmont drank.

"A brandy will do nicely, thank you," Gerard replied.

Sir Rolf motioned to a servant standing nearby and ordered the brandy, adding, "and bring some biscuits also. I have worked up a fearful appetite, and I am sure my guest could use some refreshment after his journey. We shall make it a proper tea without the tea."

They made pleasantries until after the brandy and biscuits had been deposited on the table and Sir Rolf had dismissed the servant. He held up his glass in a half salute, downed the brandy in two swallows, poured more from the decanter on the table, then turned to Gerard. "What is this mysterious business you have with me, Egmont?"

Gerard could feel the color rushing to his face. Now that he was actually here, confronting Caradoc, his courage was beginning to fail. Also, he considered Sir Rolf's attitude somewhat patronizing, and he did not like that, particularly coming from one who he hoped would soon be his brother-in-law.

"I shall get to the point at once," he said, not wishing to prolong this encounter any longer than absolutely necessary. "If memory serves me correctly, you offered for my sister some years back, did you not?"

"I did," Sir Rolf said, smiling. He had lost the game; never could he have guessed the nature of young Egmont's business. Now, however, it was becoming increasingly evident what that business was. "Your father told me at the time—let me see . . . damme! . . . it must have been nearly three years ago—that your sister was too young."

"She is older now," Gerard said unnecessarily. "In six weeks she will be twenty." He waited, hoping Sir Rolf would say something. What he honestly wanted was for the man to spring up enthusiastically and offer for Jocelyn again.

Sir Rolf, however, now anticipated his visitor and had no intention whatever of playing into his hands. He wanted the sister for a wife, would do almost anything to get her, but it would never do to let this eager young man know that. He remained silent, observing with inward glee the nerve-wracking effect of the silence upon the younger man.

"W-would you like to offer for her again?" Gerard finally blurted.

"At what price?" Sir Rolf asked calmly.

Gerard jumped up so quickly that his chair overturned behind him. "Sir!" he cried, "what do you mean by that? You are insulting both my sister and me as well as the good name of Egmont."

Sir Rolf smiled maddeningly at him. "No insult intended. Though I think even if one were, you would not call me out. Sit down, Egmont, and cease your outbursts. They are entirely unnecessary, for I believe we understand each other perfectly. You know that I—at one time, at least—wanted to marry your sister, and I know that you now want me to marry her. The question is: Why do you want me to marry Miss Egmont? And the first answer that comes to my mind is money. So I am asking: How much?"

"I . . . er . . . you have . . ." Gerard began stammering.

"Oh, get to the point, man!"

"We have fallen on hard times, my sister and I, since the death of our father," Gerard began, hesitated, then went on. "There is not enough of our inheritance left to keep up house and grounds." He waited again, and when his only answer was silence, he added, "Or the household staff . . . or ourselves."

"Ran through it all in a hurry, did you?" Sir Rolf said, an almost benign smile lighting his face.

"Our fortune was a very modest one," Gerard said, staring down at the table.

"And I have heard talk both here and in London of your romance with the games of chance." Sir Rolf stroked the top of his balding head thoughtfully. "I have seen your sister only once, and since that was many years ago, she was but a child. Should I not know how she has turned out as a young woman?"

The one time he had seen her had been at a party at Egmont House when he was still accepted by the local gentry. Jocelyn had been about twelve or thirteen and, he remembered, a little beauty even then. It was on the basis of that memory that he had offered for her two and a half years ago. Unfortunately, he had not had so much as a glimpse of her that day.

"She is lovely," Gerard said quickly, "both to behold and in her disposition."

Sir Rolf nodded. "I shall take your word for that.

What does she think of me . . . or of her brother coming to me?"

"She does not know that I am here, and as for what she thinks of you, I have never heard her mention your name."

Sir Rolf began laughing. The deal was to be even more mercenary than he had imagined. He could tell young Egmont was extremely uncomfortable now and that made him laugh all the more.

"All right, Egmont," he said after several minutes, watching the younger man squirm. "What I shall do is to have my barrister draw up papers stating that I shall take over the upkeep of Egmont House and give you a monthly allowance as well, beginning the day your sister and I are married. Come back in a month and I shall have the agreement here, ready for your signature. I shall also have a check for you, but the check must be held until after the wedding ceremony. Meanwhile, I trust I have your permission to call upon Miss Egmont. Er . . . I do not seem to remember her name."

"Jocelyn," Gerard said, thinking quickly that if Jocelyn knew about the bargain, or even set eyes upon Sir Rolf before the agreement was signed, all would be lost. "But, no," he said, "you do not have my permission to call at Egmont House until after the papers are signed."

"Are you questioning my honor?" Sir Rolf was turning red with rage.

"Indeed not!" Gerard said hastily. "It is just that I think it would be better for all concerned to wait. You see . . ."

"No need to explain," Sir Rolf said, his anger diminishing. "I believe I understand. You are afraid your sister might prove somewhat reluctant. You are right in supposing that I want to do nothing to incur her displeasure, for having a reluctant bride is not a fate that appeals to me. Now, give me your hand on our bargain, and we shall each go our separate way and do what we must."

They shook hands and Gerard left. Sir Rolf sat back down at the table, his hand unconscioiusly rubbing his rotund stomach. Good news came sometimes when least expected, and from sources least likely. He knew from talk about the county that the Egmont girl was a beauty, and the fact that she had no dowry bothered him not at all. She was of the gentry and more than acceptable as the mistress of Caradoc Court and the mother of his heir.

He poured himself another brandy and began laughing loudly. It had been years since he was so happy.

Three days after securing Gerard Egmont's signature on the marriage agreement, Sir Rolf was still a vessel of good humor. The blessings which came to most men early in life were later coming to him, but they were coming at long last, he mused. And he had a decided advantage over most men, for he had lived exactly as he pleased all his life, and his drinking habits and debauchery had not, in the long run, hindered him from getting a proper bride. Oh, for a while it had seemed as though he was going to die without an heir and that everything would go to Edward, including the title which he, as older son, had inherited from their father. That thought had caused him many a day of worrying, many a sleepless night.

But now it had all come out exactly right. He chuckled again as he remembered the look on Gerard's face as he signed the agreement.

"You understand all the terms perfectly, I trust," he had said to Gerard. "You and the bride are to come here on the morning of the wedding. The ceremony will take place at noon in the chapel here. I shall see to getting a vicar to perform the rites. Immediately the ceremony is over, we shall repair to the great hall to drink a toast, and after that, you are free to go."

From the way Sir Rolf said it, Gerard knew that he was not only free to go, but would be expected to go at once. "About the wedding guests . . ." he began.

"You are not to give any part of the wedding a thought," Sir Rolf said quickly. "I shall take care of everything. I surmise you are still not of a mind to let me see my bride-to-be?"

Gerard flinched visibly. "Uh . . . well, I think that is best. I . . ."

"You do not need to explain," Sir Rolf said. "I understand quite well." It was obvious to him that Gerard expected his sister to have strenuous objections to the marriage, and it was also obvious that, even though the agreement had been signed, it would behoove him to go along with Gerard's wishes until after the ceremony.

"When are you going to tell your sister of her approaching good fortune?" he asked with a laugh.

"Tomorrow, I think."

Now, Sir Rolf was in his sitting room, awaiting Edward, whom he had summoned. He was so filled with glee at the prospect of telling Edward about the forthcoming nuptials that he was smiling to himself, and every now and then a gurgle of laughter came to the surface and spilled over. All these years Edward had thought the land, the title, the house, everything would be his someday, and now he was about to find out that the rest of his life would be no different from that which had gone before. He would spend it managing the estate as he had done for the past six years, and even though Edward pretended to like the job, Sir Rolf was positive that it was all just that—pretense; no one could enjoy being little more than an overseer.

Sir Rolf could not have told exactly why he so thoroughly detested his brother, but any member of his household staff, all of whom liked and respected Edward, could have. Edward was the exact opposite of Rolf, both in appearance and nature. Eighteen years his brother's junior, Edward was tall and straight and had a head of thick black hair and features much more finely honed than his brother's. He was a quiet and thoughtful man, where Rolf was rambunctious; he preferred working about the estate to traveling about the countryside, and reading to cavorting around at parties and balls. Shy and retiring in nature, he was, according to the few who knew him well, strong in character where his brother was weak.

The reason for Sir Rolf's dislike of Edward—the only reason that Sir Rolf would admit to himself—was not known to anyone, and Sir Rolf intended to keep it that way. It was a secret he expected to carry to his grave. Now that he was going to marry and produce an heir, it would be much easier for him to keep that secret. Now that there would be no possibility of Edward's ever inheriting Caradoc Court, Sir Rolf could, perhaps, even afford to be a bit kinder to Edward. Treat him with the same benign objectivity with which he treated the servants.

A feeling of pure joy spread through him as a new idea for Edward occurred to him, and at that moment Edward himself appeared in the doorway.

"You wanted to see me?" he asked.

"I did indeed," Sir Rolf boomed jovially. "Sit down, Edward. We need to have a little talk."

With a somewhat bemused expression on his face, Edward sat down opposite his brother. It was unusual for him to see Rolf even in passing, let alone to be summoned by him. As long as the management of the estate was well run, Edward knew that Rolf had no desire to see him. Nor, for that matter, was he ever anxious to run into Rolf. He was keenly aware of the fact that he and Rolf had nothing in common except their home and name, and he was also aware of the way his brother felt about him, although he was not sure why. He had speculated early in life that Rolf's dislike was due to the great difference in their ages, that perhaps Rolf resented the way their father had made Edward his favorite from the time he was a baby.

Although Caradoc Court, along with Sir Charles Caradoc's title, went to the elder son, it had been specified in Sir Charles's will that Edward was to make his home there as long as he desired and that he was to draw funds from the estate for as long as he lived.

Edward sat quietly, waiting for his brother to state his business with him. He had learned it was far better to wait and gauge Rolf's moods than to make comment and incur his wrath if he chanced to be in a bad mood, which was often. On occasion even a statement about the weather had been known to put Sir Rolf into quite a temper, although right now his brother seemed to be studying him with an expression of considerable amusement in his eyes.

"I have news for you, Edward," he said at last. "I plan to be married soon."

"Congratulations, brother. Indeed, my sincere felicitations! I am delighted for you," Edward said at once. "Am I acquainted with the lady?"   ,

"I think not. Her name is Jocelyn Egmont. She is the daughter of the late Harold Egmont who lived some distance from here."

"I have heard of him, of course. A good and honorable man. When will the nuptials take place?"

"In a fortnight," Sir Rolf said, enjoying to the fullest the look of surprise on Edward's face. "We shall be married here in the chapel. I have already begun making the arrangements for the wedding."

"Is that not a bit unusual?" Edward asked. "Not only

the short time of betrothal, but also that you should be the one to make the arrangements?"

"In this instance, no. According to Miss Egmont's brother, the family has fallen on hard times, and he desires to have his sister married as soon as possible. Under the circumstances, it is naturally better for me to make the arrangements and to have the wedding here."

Although Edward had been surprised at his brother's announcement, it had hardly been stunning. The last statement, however, was. It would appear that Rolf was buying a bride, and from what he himself had heard of the Egmont family, it did not seem likely that a daughter of Harold Egmont would consent to being bought. But he refrained from commenting on this. "Again, my felicitations," he said. "It will be good to have a mistress of Caradoc Court. I have never known what it is like to have a woman in the house, as our mother died when I was born."

Sir Rolf winced noticeably. "Yes," was all he said. Then he remembered the idea which had occurred to him just before Edward came in. "I shall be needing the entire west wing of the house for my wife and myself, so I suggest you move your quarters to another place—possibly the east wing near your office would suffice."

The servants' quarters, Edward thought. And it was entirely unnecessary that he move, because there was more than enough room in the west wing for several families. Oh, well, it made little difference where he slept; he could be comfortable in the east wing, and then too, it might be just as well for him to put that much distance between himself and the newlyweds. "That is agreeable with me," he said. "I shall remove my things at once so you can begin preparing the rooms for your bride."

Sir Rolf was crestfallen. His disappointment in Edward's reaction, both to the announcement of his approaching marriage and to his order that Edward remove himself to the servants' part of the house, was bitter indeed. He was sure that Edward was seething inside and was simply not showing it because he wanted to frustrate his brother. However, he had one more blow to administer, nothing to compare with the other two, but at least one which should possibly put Edward into a fine pique.

"I have a small favor to ask of you," he said.

"I shall be happy to oblige you in any way I can," Edward said.

"I have a betrothal ring for Miss Egmont, one of my mother's rings that I should like her to have, and with all the preparations to be made, I have not the time to go to Egmont House. Since I would not like to entrust such an errand to a servant—it would not be the thing, you know—I should like you to take the ring to her."

Edward threw his hands up involuntarily. "Surely you can spare the day it would take to travel to and from Egmont House. If you left at dawn you could be back by sunset the same day. Your bride-to-be assuredly would rather have the ring from her betrothed than from his brother."

"No." Sir Rolf was adamant. "There is no time, no time at all, and I should like her to have the ring as soon as possible. Therefore, I suggest you go tomorrow." He stood up and went to a nearby table, picked up a small package, and gave it to Edward. It was obvious that he intended to say no more; his business with his brother was finished.

With deep misgivings, Edward took the package, dreading its delivery more than he had ever dreaded anything.

At best, it could only prove a very awkward situation. At worst . . . That depended, of course, on the attitude of Rolf's bride-to-be.

Three

Rain and unseasonably cold weather continued for four days, thus delaying Edward's journey to Egmont House to deliver his brother's betrothal ring to Jocelyn. With each passing day, Edward dreaded the errand more, because as he had time to give more thought to Rolf's approaching marriage, he found his chief reaction was one of disapproval. What else could it be, he reasoned, when it was so obvious the Egmont girl was being bought, purchased as one would purchase a trinket? A few discreet questions of the most trusted members of the household staff had given Edward a good bit of information about the Egmonts. Although Harold Egmont had been an upstanding, honest man, his offspring were quite obviously not cut from the same cloth, Edward decided. The boy, Gerard, was revealed to Edward as a gambler, an unprincipled wastrel, and his sister, Jocelyn . . . well, it was certainly apparent enough what she was by what she was doing. Rolf's reputation throughout the countryside was no secret to Edward and neither was the fact that Rolf had been trying for years to find a bride from the Polite World.

The biggest surprise to Edward, however, was the fact that an otherwise proper young lady would allow herself

35

to be bought by someone with Rolf's reputation . . .
even a young lady in impoverished circumstances. Had
he been Miss Jocelyn Egmont, Edward thought, he
should have preferred poverty, dire need, even starvation,
to marriage to Rolf.

By the time thin rays of sunlight showed themselves
on the fifth day, Edward had worked up an active dislike
for the girl who would be his sister-in-law. He was glad
now that Rolf had insisted he move to another wing of
the house; he wanted as little as possible to do with Rolf
and his mercenary wife.

He set out in the early morning, noting that Regent,
his new pinto horse, was much more eager for the trip
than he himself. The gelding had not been exercised
during the rainy days and could hardly be held back
now. Finally, Edward gave him his head and let him set
his own pace; thus they arrived at Egmont House somewhat sooner than Edward had intended. The servant who
came to the door informed him that the Egmonts were
at table having their midday meal and asked him to wait
in the circular hallway.

"It is Miss Egmont I am here to see, not her brother,"
Edward said. "You may say that Edward Caradoc of
Caradoc Court is calling." His dislike of his errand had
increased steadily as he had neared his destination, and
now that he was actually here, he had no desire to see
either of the Egmonts, certainly not both of them. Even
had he not heard of Gerard's weaknesses, he would have
had no use whatever for a man who would allow his
sister to marry someone of Rolf's reputation.

He looked around the circular entry, noting the gold
mirror at the end of the circular staircase, the matching
Roman chairs by the doorway which obviously led into
a large parlor, the delicate shades of green and gold in
the Persian rug upon which he was standing, the tall,

beautifully made clock by the doorway which led to the back part of the house, and nodded approvingly. The room was furnished with impeccable taste, and there was no reason for him to suppose that the rest of the house was otherwise. It was too bad that the brother and sister residing here now did not display the same good taste as their parents or whatever ancestors had built and furnished this beautiful old house.

The servant returned and informed him that Miss Egmont would see him and that he was to join her and her brother in the dining room.

Edward followed the servant to a large room with a long table and noticed that the woman, instead of sitting at the foot of the table, sat at her brother's right. The brother, at the head of the table, rose when Edward entered, held out his hand, and said, "I thought at first when you were announced that the servant had made a mistake and that it was Sir Rolf who was here, but I bid you welcome, sir, and I am happy to make your acquaintance."

Edward shook Gerard's hand and bowed slightly. "Thank you," he said. He had almost added, making his manners, "And I the same," but had not, deciding he could not be that much the hypocrite. His eyes went immediately to the young woman. She, apparently, could not decide whether to rise to make her caller welcome or remain seated. She chose the latter and stared at Edward, her blue-gray eyes wide and inquiring.

Edward's first impression was that her face had such an innocent, almost childlike look that she could not possibly be guilty of all the base and low tricks of which he had been accusing her in his mind during his ride to Egmont House. His second impression, after carefully studying Jocelyn as a whole—her lustrous black hair, her creamy complexion, the proud, almost defiant tilt of her head—was that she was perfectly beautiful and a most interesting woman as well, one whom, had he met her under different circumstances and in a different place, he would have wanted to know much better. But then he remembered the circumstances and his errand, and his original opinion returned and his thought was: Well, at least Rolf is going to get his money's worth.

"My sister, Jocelyn," Gerard was saying, and Edward bowed.

The butler had placed a plate at Gerard's left, across from Jocelyn, and Gerard said, "You will join us, of course," and without waiting for an answer began to heap a pungent-smelling stew upon the plate from a large silver tureen in front of him.

Edward had not realized how hungry he was. "Thank you," he said. "I have had a long ride this morning. Food will be most welcome."

"What brings you to this part of the county?" Gerard asked, and Edward noticed for the first time that the young man's face was puckered with worry lines, as though he was expecting bad news. Edward almost laughed as it occurred to him what Gerard must be thinking: that he, Edward, had come to say that Rolf had decided not to go through with the marriage. What a delicious joke it would be on these two fortune hunters if only it were true!

"I have come on behalf of my brother," Edward said slowly, pausing and relishing the stricken expression that was beginning to appear on Gerard's face. He glanced across at Jocelyn, expecting to see much the same expression, but she was merely looking at him inquiringly, her lovely eyes narrowed as she waited for the answer to the unasked question.

"Yes, what is it, man?" Gerard said finally, fidgeting in his chair. "I trust nothing has happened to Sir Rolf."

"Nothing except that he is frightfully busy now making plans for the approaching nuptials," Edward said. He could see the relief spread over Gerard's face like a player's mask with an upturned, smiling mouth. As for Jocelyn, she immediately looked down at her plate and he could not see enough of her face to tell how great her relief was.

Edward reached into his pocket and brought forth the small box and pushed it across the table toward Jocelyn. Hardly the way to present a lady with a betrothal ring, he thought, but after all, everything considered . . .

"My brother wanted me to bring you this," he said. "It belonged to our mother, and Rolf wants you to have it."

Jocelyn looked at the little box as though it contained a viper. She did not lift a hand to touch it. Could she really be so provoked because Rolf himself did not bring it? Edward wondered.

"Well, open it, you silly girl," Gerard said after a minute or two. And then for Edward's benefit, "My sister is not accustomed to receiving gifts . . . and also she is getting excited, and a little nervous, I suspect, as the wedding date draws nearer."

Still Jocelyn did not touch the box. "What is it?" she asked, her voice almost a whisper.

"It is a betrothal ring," Edward said. "Rolf asked that I relay his regrets to you that he was unable to bring the ring himself." It was totally untrue; Rolf had said nothing of the kind, but it seemed to Edward that he should cater to at least a few of the social amenities. He reached across the table, picked up the box and opened it himself, taking the ring from its tiny velvet cushion and holding it out to Jocelyn. It was a large ruby in a setting of small diamonds, a valuable ring which probably was beautiful on a large hand, but Edward found the ring too gaudy for his taste and, looking at Jocelyn's small hands and long tapered fingers, thought it would look atrocious on her. Somehow, the ruby did not seem to be the right jewel for her.

She stared at the ring as though she had no idea what it was or what she should do with it, and Edward was determined that he was not going to go around the table and put it on her. That was Rolf's job, and if he did not choose to do it, the girl could put the ring on herself.

Gerard stood up suddenly, took the ring, then reached for Jocelyn's hand and put it on. Jocelyn stared at her brother for a minute, then looked down at the ring. "How right that you should be the one to place it on my finger, Gerard," she said softly.

Edward concentrated on his food then, wanting to finish his meal and get away as soon as possible. He had completed his errand and he saw no reason to prolong his visit with these two.

"If my horse has been seen to, I must be on my way," he said to Gerard.

"So soon?" Gerard asked. "Why not wait until to-morrow and give us a chance to get better acquainted?"

"I am afraid I had better be leaving," he said, "in the event that the rain begins again. I should not like to be caught halfway between here and Caradoc Court."

Edward summoned the butler and told him to have the stableboy bring around Mr. Caradoc's horse, and then the three of them rose from the table.

Jocelyn held out her hand to Edward and said, "Good-day to you, Mr. Caradoc," and walked quickly out of the room before either he or Gerard could utter a word.

Deuce take it, Edward thought, at least she could have thanked him for making the long trip to bring her the ring. But then, her lack of manners went right along with everything else he had thought of her.

Gerard, obviously embarrassed, said quickly, "You must forgive Jocelyn. The poor girl has worked up a nasty case of nerves. I suppose the fact that she has no women to counsel with, except for her abigail, makes this time of preparation unusually trying for her."

"I understand," Edward said, and wondered what Gerard would say if he knew exactly how much Edward *did* understand.

Gerard walked outside with Edward and stood beside him as the stableboy helped him mount. "Now that we are to be related, in a manner of speaking, we must get to know one another," Gerard said. "You must come for a longer visit."

"Thank you," Edward said, applying his heels to Regent's flanks, causing the horse to start off in a canter. He could not get away from Egmont House and its occupants fast enough to suit him. He did, however, as another concession to good manners, turn in his saddle and raise his hand to Gerard as he and Regent went though the wide iron gate.

All he could think of during the long ride back was the thoroughly unpleasant prospect of having Jocelyn rule the roost as mistress of Caradoc Court.

Jocelyn sat at her bedroom window and watched Edward Caradoc mount his brown-and-white horse and ride out the gate. She looked down at her hand, quickly removed the ring, and placed it carefully in the little silver vault on the bureau which contained the few pieces of good jewelry which had belonged to her mother and grandmother. She felt completely numb.

It was not a new feeling, for after her first histrionics she had felt this way ever since Gerard had told her she must marry Sir Rolf. In the days and nights since then she had thought of nothing but ways in which she might escape this abominable fate, but each way that came to mind had to be discarded as either impractical or impossible. Finally, she was resigned. There was nothing she could do but go through with the hideous ceremony which, as far as she was concerned, would have absolutely no meaning.

Just last night in one final attempt to bring Gerard to his senses she had said to him, "You may take me to Caradoc Court if you wish, but when the time comes to say my vows, I shall stand as though mute. Never will I promise to love, honor and obey that man! The ceremony will be invalid."

Gerard glared at her. "And do you know what will happen to me then? Sir Rolf will call me out. It will mean sure death for me. Is that what you want, Jocelyn? To see me murdered?"

"I would do it myself if I could," she had retorted.

But, of course, she could not, nor would she if she could. Despising what Gerard had done to her was one thing, but causing or sanctioning his death was entirely different. He was, after all, still her brother, her only living relative.

For the sake of Gerard's safety, his very life, she would have to go through with the marriage in spite of the fact that he did not deserve that much consideration from her after what he had done.

She turned toward the door as Irva entered the bedroom. "He has gone, miss," she said. "Just this minute past the gate."

"I saw," Jocelyn said. "Did you get a peek at him?"

"That I did, miss. When I heard who was here I went straight to the kitchen and Cook gave me a look through the pantry door. Aye, and it's a real pity he is not the one you are marrying instead of his brother. Handsome, he is, oh! And much closer to your own age."

"I did not care for him at all," Jocelyn said. "I thought

him . . . abrupt, almost rude." The words came to her just then as she thought about him. All during the meal she had been trying to decide what it was about him that she did not like. "And it was perfectly clear that he liked me . . . and Gerard . . . even less. I do not believe his brother could be much worse."

"I hope not, miss," Irva said in a tone that implied she had prior knowledge that the brother was a hundred times worse.

There was a knock at the door and Gerard entered. "Irva . . ." he began.

"Yes, I was just going downstairs," Irva interrupted. She was finding it unusually hard to be nice to Mr. Gerard these days.

As soon as she had left and closed the door behind her, Gerard crossed the room to Jocelyn and took her left hand, staring at it and then drawing back. "Where is the ring? Why are you not wearing it?"

Jocelyn shrugged. "I have put it in the case with the other jewels. I shall never wear it."

"But you must!" Gerard cried, anxiety causing perspiration to break out on his forehead. "What will Sir Rolf think if you do not wear his ring?"

"I do not care in the least what he thinks," Jocelyn said. "I do not think it was part of your contract with him that I wear a ring, and I would not wear it in any case. It is a monstrous piece. The stone is so large that it resembles paste; it is cheap-looking. And it is much too large for me."

"Perhaps we can have it cut down, but I doubt if it can be done before the wedding," Gerard said.

"I will not wear that ring no matter what you do to it," Jocelyn told him firmly.

"I trust you will be more reasonable when it comes to wearing a wedding ring," Gerard snapped.

Jocelyn stared at him. This was something she had not considered. She would, of course, have to wear a wedding ring—unless she could arrange to lose it. She would give that idea more thought later.

"How are the fittings for your wedding dress going?" Gerard asked. "I saw the seamstress leave the house yesterday. She will be finished in time, I trust."

"I suppose so."

"Jocelyn, I am dashed if I can understand you." Gerard glared at her. "The wealthiest man in the county offers for you and you act as though you have been grossly insulted. Then his brother comes here to bring you a beautiful ring and *you* behave insultingly toward the brother. I should not be surprised if Sir Rolf decided to call off the whole thing."

"Oh, do you think he might!" Jocelyn cried delightedly, the undertone of sarcasm almost not discernible.

Gerard shook his head in anger and frustration and stalked out of the room.

Jocelyn went back to the window and looked toward the gate. Edward Caradoc and his horse had long since disappeared, but for the moment she could not get Sir Rolf's brother out of her mind.

When she had first heard of Edward, of Sir Rolf's dislike of him, she had thought . . . had hoped . . . that Edward might possibly be her ally at Caradoc Court, a friend in an enemy camp. But now she had met Edward and knew that her hope had been futile. He had obviously disliked her on sight, perhaps even before he had seen her. He had treated her coldly from the moment he had entered the dining room. He had been, she decided, no more civil toward her than the rules of common politeness demanded and probably, if he had had his way, would not even have been that. There had been no warmth in his eyes at all as he scrutinized her carefully; he might as well have been examining horseflesh .to be sure it measured up.

Yet . . . had she met him at another time, in another place, and in a more casual situation, she would have liked him. Of that she was sure. He was extremely attractive—handsome, actually—and beneath that cold, aloof exterior, there might possibly lurk a warm, charming human being. Had she met him in different circumstances . . .

But there was no use in thinking such thoughts now.

She went to the bureau and took the key to the little silver vault out of the top drawer. Opening the case, she removed the ring and took it to the window where she studied it carefully.

No, she had not been mistaken before. The ring was tastelessly showy, garish. The sun shining through the ruby caused little red dots to be reflected across her palm. Like drops of blood, she thought as she closed her hand.

There was no question in her mind: The hideous ring was indicative of the hideous future she would have at Caradoc Court.

Four

The persistent tugging at her arm finally awakened Jocelyn. She sat up and looked at Irva who was standing beside her bed with a breakfast tray.

"It is time for you to be up, Miss Jocelyn. Sir Rolf's carriage already waits outside."

Jocelyn groaned and fell back on the pillow.

"Would it be amiss if I offered you felicitations on your birthday?" Irva asked.

"Not in the least," Jocelyn said, "as long as you do not wish me many happy returns of the day."

Today was the terrible, much dreaded day. Sir Rolf had sent his carriage yesterday so that the bride and her party might leave in the early morning for Caradoc Court where the wedding would take place at noon. Jocelyn was to be accompanied by Gerard, who was to take his departure shortly after the ceremony, and by Irva, who would be allowed to remain at Caradoc Court as Jocelyn's abigail.

At the foot of Jocelyn's bed were a small trunk and two portmanteaux containing her entire wardrobe which had been packed yesterday morning. Yesterday afternoon she had gone from room to room in Egmont House, studying each room as carefully as though she never expected to see it again. She looked at family portraits, at heirlooms purchased on the continent; stopping at each window, she tried to memorize the scene outside so she could call it up like a picture in her mind whenever she felt homesick.

At last she went out to the rose garden where Harold Egmont had spent so many hours in happy labor with his beloved flowers. It was then that she broke down for the first time since the day Gerard had told her she must marry Sir Rolf. How could she bear to leave Egmont House and the gardens, both of which held so many memories of her parents, her past? This was her home, and she loved it dearly. Never would she feel about another place as she did about this one. No matter how beautiful Caradoc Court was, it could not replace Egmont House in her heart.

Now, as she dressed for the journey, she looked around her room and shivered involuntarily as she thought of having to share a room with a man she could remember having seen only once in her life, a man her father had ordered away from Egmont House.

As Irva slipped the dark blue traveling suit over her mistress's head, Jocelyn thought of the white satin dress, packed on top of everything else, in the trunk. She would be putting on that dress in just a few hours. "I wish I could die right now," she said softly.

"Oh, no, miss!" Irva said. "Never that! Perhaps your new life will be much better than you think. You may even grow fond of Sir Rolf in time."

Irva's words, perfunctorily spoken, sounded unconvincing even to Irva.

When Jocelyn was ready, the two of them descended the wide, curving stairway and walked outside to the ornate carriage as though they were going to meet a death sentence.

The May sunshine was bright and the day was warm, and Jocelyn scanned the familiar countryside from the carriage as they rode along. Gerard's horse was tied to the back of the carriage, as he planned to ride home. If only, Jocelyn thought, she could leap on that horse when they arrived at their destination and disappear, leaving Gerard to be the one stranded at Caradoc Court. That thought brought the first faint smile to her face.

She continued to gaze at the countryside, a last loving look at the beech groves and the patches of bluebells which appeared like deep, blue lakes. She breathed deeply to inhale the fragrance of the sweet-scented hyacinths growing beneath the trees, and in the distance she saw the rolling, unbelievably green hills and fields where herds of cows and flocks of sheep grazed peacefully.

Soon they were passing through the village where each thatched cottage had a tiny garden blazing with the colors of bright spring flowers.

In the country again, they continued on for an hour or so until they reached The Cloak and Candle Inn where they stopped for refreshment and to rest the horses.

It was eleven o'clock before they were in sight of Caradoc Court, and Jocelyn's first look at her new home filled her heart with even more despair. From the avenue leading to the house, she could see only one side of the house, the side which contained the chapel and the entryway to the courtyard. But the many giant trees growing around the house and the forest behind cast the whole area in the darkest shade, giving an air of gloom unequaled by any Jocelyn had ever experienced before. It was all she could do to keep from jumping from the carriage and throwing herself under its wheels. She closed her eyes rather than look longer at the dismal scene.

"Well, here we are at last," Gerard remarked as the

carriage halted. "And there is Edward Caradoc to greet us."

Jocelyn opened her eyes. They were inside the courtyard. The carriage had stopped before the west wing of the house and Edward Caradoc was coming down the graystone steps. Where, Jocelyn wondered, was the happy groom? It seemed logical to her, as well as good manners, that he should be the one to hand her down from the carriage and welcome her to her new home. Perhaps, she thought, he is as unmannerly as his brother proved himself to be when he visited Egmont House.

Gerard, however, guessed immediately why it was Edward and not Rolf who greeted them. So far the plans had progressed with no untoward incidents, and Sir Rolf would not tempt fate by permitting even the slightest chance of something going wrong before the ceremony. He would greet his bride at the altar in the chapel and not before.

"Good day, Mr. Egmont," Edward was saying to Gerard, who had sprung from the carriage, "and to you, Miss Egmont," he continued as Gerard turned and helped Jocelyn down. "I know you will both want to go to your quarters immediately since it is less than an hour before the wedding ceremony. If you will follow me, please . . ."

Not a word of welcome, Jocelyn thought as she and Gerard and Irva went with Edward into the house. They were followed by four of the Caradoc servants bringing the luggage.

The house, or what part Jocelyn could see from the long hallways, was as gloomy inside as out. They stopped in front of one door which Edward opened. "You may use this room, Mr. Egmont," he said. "And your rooms, Miss Egmont, are here." He opened the door across the hall onto a small sitting room. "Your abigail will have the room at the end of the hall. You may ring for the servants, and anything you need or want will be brought at once." He pointed to the bell-cord by the fireplace in the sitting room.

"Thank you," Jocelyn said, her voice sounding hoarse and like that of a stranger.

"As you know," Edward went on, "we shall all meet in the chapel at noon for the nuptials. My brother sends you his greetings and says he will see you then." He made a slight bow and left them.

Jocelyn and Irva made no comment as they looked around the apartment. Beyond the sitting room was a large bedroom, dominated by a huge four-poster, canopied bed, and just off the bedroom was a dressing room.

Jocelyn could not take her eyes off the monstrous bed, the reality of what she was doing—what she was being forced to do—finally overcoming her. She burst into sudden, uncontrollable tears.

"Now, now, miss, you mustn't do that." Irva tried to comfort her. "You mustn't have red, tearful eyes at your wedding. And we must get ready at once." She went back to the sitting room where the servants had deposited the trunk and portmanteaux and took the wedding dress from the trunk. She pulled the bell-cord and when a maid-servant appeared at the door she gave her the dress, saying, "The wrinkles must be ironed from the skirt and the dress brought back as quickly as you can. Hurry, girl!"

Jocelyn had stopped crying and was staring in frightened wonder at the ceiling. In each corner and along one side of the wall were the most terrible gargoyles she had ever seen. Even the grinning ones, those supposedly with a happy expression, seemed to have an evil leer, and the frowning faces were so horrible that she could compare them with nothing she had ever seen before. It was as though she had awakened suddenly to find that the appall-

ing, terrifying nightmare she had been having was all
true.

She cried out one time, half-scream, half-sob, and
collapsed into the nearest chair; Irva came from the
next room to minister to the distraught girl.

Standing beside Gerard, Edward looked at the backs
of the bride and groom as they knelt in front of the altar.
The entire ceremony lasted slightly less than fifteen minutes, and it was now almost over. Rolf and Jocelyn were
kneeling on a white satin cushion for the final blessing
from the vicar. All Edward could think of was that
the stone floor of the chapel was so cold that his legs were
beginning to ache.

He did not know the vicar, John Bedwain. Rolf had
told him last night that the vicar from the village, Henry
Lawrence, was indisposed and that he, Rolf, had had to
go to great trouble to obtain another vicar from some
distance. Apparently the new vicar was performing as
well as Lawrence could have, for the ceremony, to all
outward appearances, was going perfectly.

Edward had not been able to hear Jocelyn when she
repeated her vows, so low had she spoken, but Rolf's
voice had been strong enough for both of them. He had
roared out the words, his voice revealing his high good
humor.

Edward could not tell what kind of mood the bride
was in, for her veil was so heavy he could not even
distinguish her features beneath it when she had come into
the chapel on Gerard's arm. He supposed, however, that
her mood would match Rolf's. Why not, since they were
both getting exactly what they wanted: Rolf, a wife from
the Polite World to be the mother of his heir; Jocelyn, a
tremendous house and a large staff of servants over which
she could be mistress, and a title and fortune as well. No

wonder she had stood so erect and proud as they exchanged vows.

Another thought came to Edward then. This girl was,
after all, his sister-in-law now, and fortune hunter and
whatever else she might be was best forgotten. Although
there would be a great distance between them, the same
roof would shelter them both, and it would make both
their lives more pleasant if they could at least give the
appearance of getting along.

The vicar gave the benediction and the couple turned
from the altar. Rolf, who had not seen his bride until her
brother had escorted her to his side at the altar, looked
almost like a vulture, Edward thought, as he pulled the
veil back from Jocelyn's face and kissed her cheek
greedily.

For a moment, it appeared to Edward that Jocelyn
flinched under that loud, smacking kiss, but he supposed
that he was mistaken, for almost immediately she smiled
and then lowered her head demurely.

She was breathtakingly beautiful. The clouds of white
net and lace around her face only accentuated her coal-
black hair, and for the second time Edward was struck
by the look of childlike innocence on her face. She was
like a lamb—the thought came unbidden to Edward's
mind—a sacrificial lamb being presented to the ravenous
Rolf.

Then he realized the thought was silly, not worth considering. That girl was sacrificing nothing; she was getting
exactly what she wanted. Jocelyn and Rolf deserved each
other.

They came from the altar, Rolf holding Jocelyn's arm
firmly, and walked quickly to the back of the chapel, then
out the door.

Edward turned to Gerard, remembering the invitation
he was supposed to issue. "We are to join the bridal

couple in the great hall for the wedding breakfast," he
said.

The two of them walked past Irva and those members
of the household staff who had been invited to the wedding. Outside, Gerard said jovially to Edward, "Now
that our families are joined, you and I are brothers-in-law
. . . in a distant sort of way."

That thought gave Edward little pleasure.

Sir Rolf was a happy man. He felt happy in every bone
and fiber of his being as he held to Jocelyn's arm, leading
her across the courtyard and into the north wing of the
house where the great hall was located. She walked very
slowly, he supposed because the satin slippers were thin
and insubstantial and because she was carrying the long
white train of the dress tucked under her right arm.

"A beautiful wedding," he said to his new wife, "and
you are the most beautiful of brides."

She was looking down at the ground as they walked
and made no answer. No matter, there would be time for
them to talk, to get acquainted, after the wedding breakfast
when Gerard would go back to Egmont House and Rolf
would send Edward about his business. He would have
Jocelyn all to himself then, and the prospect caused the
palms of his hands to perspire as his excitement mounted.

Everything was turning out so much better than he had
expected. He had been afraid, up to the very last minute,
that he would have an hysterical bride on his hands. From
the things Gerard had said on his first visit and again when
he came to sign the marriage contract, Rolf had thought
that probably Jocelyn was so opposed to the marriage
that she might even throw a childish tantrum, or worse,
to show her resentment toward both her brother and
Rolf. He knew now, however, that she was not the type
for such behavior. She was a stoic, he decided, showing

no feeling whatever. Or else, she was resigned to being his wife and intended to make the best of it. After all, was being married to Sir Rolf Caradoc and being mistress of Caradoc Court such a bad fate?

For a while during the ceremony, he had been afraid she might faint, so heavily had she leaned on his arm. He had tried to see if she appeared pale, but the veil made it impossible for him to tell anything about her. For all he knew, Gerard could have been foisting off a hideous, pock-marked sister upon him.

After the first vows in the nave of the chapel when he and Jocelyn followed the vicar to the altar, he noticed that she was shaking slightly, and he was uncertain whether it was with fear or whether she was crying. By this time the whole thing was beginning to make him a little nervous. What if she suddenly became hysterical and ran screaming from the chapel? That possibility was one reason he had wanted no spectators at the wedding except for the two brothers and a few of the most trusted servants.

Then the ceremony was over, and he had raised her veil from her face. So great had been his relief that he had actually felt weak for a moment. She was magnificent of face as well as a fine figure of a woman. She did appear a little pale, but anyone swathed in so much white would look pale. He had planted a resounding kiss on her cheek, thinking that as soon as he got her outside the chapel, away from so many curious eyes, he would kiss her properly.

Dizzy with happiness, he guided her into the great hall, stopped as soon as they were inside the door, and took her in his arms, planting his lips firmly upon hers.

She stiffened in his arms and he felt her resistance even before she began trying to push him away. "Please . . ." she whispered, struggling free of him.

He looked around and thought he knew the reason for her reluctance. Standing behind the long, massive oak table were four servants in livery waiting to serve the wedding breakfast. Later, he thought. There would be time later . . .

He went across the vast room to the table and nodded in approval. It was laden with six candlelabra and every conceivable kind of food and wine. Hugo, the butler, in whose charge Sir Rolf had left the task of preparing the celebration, had done well. It did seem strange, however—the tremendous room, the long, long table, and only four places set. But now that he was no longer apprehensive, he could make plans for a large party, a ball even, perhaps within the next fortnight, to give his marriage the celebration it deserved.

He seated his bride beside him at the head of the table. "Today, my dear, I want you here beside me," he said. He nodded toward the foot of the table. "You can take your rightful place when the table is filled with guests."

Gerard and Edward entered at that moment, and Edward hurried to Rolf. "The vicar, Mr. Bedwain, said he was not staying. Do you know why?"

"Certainly," Rolf said. "He had other chores to perform, another service of some kind, I believe. I told him we would detain him here no longer than necessary." What he had actually told the vicar was that he could go as soon as the ceremony was over. There had been no invitation to the wedding breakfast, therefore no question of him staying.

As soon as Edward and Gerard had taken the places set for them at table, Rolf stood up and raised his wine glass. "I want to make the first toast," he said, "to my lovely bride. Your health, madam. Your health and happiness." And, he added to himself, to the many Caradoc offspring that will come from you.

He turned the glass up and downed the wine to the last drop.

Gerard drank the toast to his sister, echoing, "Your health and happiness" after Sir Rolf. And he hoped fervently that she would have an abundance of both, for she had added much to his own happiness this day. He put his hand into his pocket and gently rubbed the check which Sir Rolf had signed. Thanks to Jocelyn—and to his own ingenuity—he would have no more worries about money. Nor, for that matter, would she. Today she had feathered a nest for both of them.

It was too bad that she did not yet realize the marvelous thing she had done by marrying Sir Rolf. But he was sure she would come around sooner or later. It was easy to see that Sir Rolf was obviously quite taken with her, for he was blathering over her like a schoolboy —or an old fool.

Gerard stood next, nodding to his new brother-in-law. "Permit me, sir," he said, picking up his glass. "I drink to your long life—and that of your heirs."

He could tell by the broad smile on Sir Rolf's face that he had pleased him immensely with the toast. Good! For a while he had been afraid none of them would ever be pleased again.

Now, looking at Jocelyn across the table, he had to admit that she was the most beautiful bride he had ever seen, though certainly not the happiest. But happiness would come for her eventually, he was sure. He concentrated upon the delicacies being heaped upon his plate and looked toward Edward whose turn it was to make a toast.

Edward, however, remained seated, saying nothing, apparently so deeply engrossed in his food that he had not another thought in his head.

The instant the meal was finished, Sir Rolf stood up. "I want to thank you for being here," he said to Gerard. "You are free to go now. The festivities are at an end. And Edward," turning to his brother, "we shall not keep you longer from your business about the estate."

Edward rose immediately, bowed to Jocelyn, and without a word to anyone, left the great hall.

"Pay no attention to him, my dear," Sir Rolf said to Jocelyn. "It may be that his nose is a little out of joint."

In that case, Gerard thought, he may make life a little difficult for Jocelyn. He had heard for years that the main reason Sir Rolf was eager to marry was so that his estate, fortune, and title would not go to his brother. It was possible that Edward's nose was more than a little out of joint!

Jocelyn stood up as Gerard approached her to say good-bye. He kissed her cheek, squeezed her hand, and whispered into her ear. "Thank you, little sister. You have kept our part of the contract, and all is well."

Jocelyn said nothing, but she gave him a look so piteous that he took her hand again and held it for a minute. Then he shook hands with the bridegroom, thanked Sir Rolf for his hospitality, and went out to the stables to get his horse and begin the long ride home.

Angry as she was with Gerard, Jocelyn thought her heart would stop beating when he left the great hall. Now she was really alone among strangers. She started toward the door as though to follow her brother, but Sir Rolf was beside her instantly, holding her by the arm.

"The party does not have to end because the guests have gone," he said. "We must now drink our private toasts to each other, and then I shall show you about your new home."

"Then I should like to change into something more

suitable," Jocelyn said. She would do anything that would get her away from him even for a few minutes. "If you will excuse me . . ."

"Ah, no," he said. "You must keep on your wedding dress for a while yet. After all, you will only have one wedding day, so you must make the most of it."

"But I feel uncomfortable. It will not take very long, then I shall return for more toasts." She had reached the door while she was talking, and she went out before he could answer.

She did not know her way through the various halls that would take her to the west wing, so she held her dress off the ground with both hands and ran across the courtyard. She was panting when she reached the apartment where Irva waited for her.

"It was a lovely wedding . . ." Irva began, but was interrupted by Jocelyn's "Quickly, Irva, help me get out of this terrible dress and then put it away somewhere so I shall never have to see it again."

"But, miss . . ."

"There must be a room somewhere that is used to store old clothes. Find it!" She had thrown the veil and headdress on the floor and now was struggling, with Irva's help, to get the dress over her head. When she was free of it, she sat in the nearest chair with a huge sigh. Irva looked at her curiously for a moment, then picked up the headdress and took it, with the dress, out of the room.

Jocelyn felt as though she had been drugged for hours and was just returning to full consciousness. The entire day, so far, had been most peculiar because from the time Irva had roused her this morning until just now when she had run from the great hall, she had felt like a play-actress acting out a part which had nothing at all to do with the real Jocelyn Egmont. It was almost as though the real Jocelyn watched the play-actress Jocelyn from a great distance, or through a veil which partially hid some of the subtleties of the drama from her view.

Now, reality had settled upon her and dispensed the qualities of the play as a sudden thought all but crushed her: She was no longer Jocelyn Egmont, she was Jocelyn Caradoc! The wife of Sir Rolf Caradoc.

Tears began coursing down her cheeks and she hastily rubbed them away with the back of her hand. She had already cried so much, and what good had it done? Now it was too late for tears, too late for anything. The wedding ceremony could not be undone.

She had leaned heavily on Gerard's arm as they entered the chapel and, for a fleeting instant, had had a clear picture of Anne Boleyn in her mind and had known exactly how the young queen felt, what had been in her thoughts as she had walked from the Tower of London across the courtyard to have her head chopped off. Then the picture had faded from her mind as she looked down the aisle of the chapel to the front where Sir Rolf stood waiting for her. As she and Gerard made their way slowly down the aisle, she did not take her eyes off her bridegroom. The veil blurred her vision some, but she was aware that Sir Rolf was leering, not merely looking, at her. Her second impression was that he was not an attractive man. He looked nothing at all like his brother, Edward. Though not completely obese, Sir Rolf carried entirely too much flesh for her taste, and his hairline had receded to the point where it was almost impossible to see any hair, excepting sideburns, from the front.

A shudder went through her and she stopped momentarily. Gerard clutched her arm more firmly and led her forward. When they reached Sir Rolf, Gerard put her arm on his. She would as soon have touched a tarantula.

Several times during the ceremony, she was aware that she trembled slightly, but each time Sir Rolf looked down at her, a little smile on his slack mouth as though to say, "I understand perfectly; it is natural for brides to be nervous." She was sure he did not realize with what extreme distaste she viewed this whole impossible charade.

Now, she rested her head on the back of the chair and her eyes inadvertently went to the horrible gargoyles. They were laughing at her, those exaggerated, misshapen faces!

She closed her eyes. She could not endure this, none of it. And the thought of Sir Rolf joining her in this room, in that huge bed . . . She wanted to start screaming and never stop. Let them put her away as a mad woman! Surely that fate could be no worse! As she herself had felt a kinship to Anne Boleyn, she now thought that Sir Rolf was much like Henry the Eighth. It was conceivable that the two men had many of the same attributes.

As terrible as the ceremony had seemed, as bad as the walk to the great hall and then the toasts, the worst moment so far had been when Gerard left her. Deep though her anger at him was, she would have forgiven him anything if he had but taken her with him back to Egmont House.

Had she imagined it or had he, there at the last, looked a little sorry for what he had done to her? When he had whispered to her . . .

She sat bolt upright in the chair, remembering his words, "Thank you, little sister. You have kept our part of the contract and all is well." Those words put an idea into her head which seemed at first preposterous, but the more she thought of it . . .

Irva returned, interrupting her thoughts. "I was shown a place where the dress might be stored," she said. "Now, what shall I get out for you to wear? I have not quite finished unpacking the trunk yet."

"Have you unpacked your own portmanteau?" Jocelyn asked.

"No, miss, not yet. I wanted to get you settled in first."

"Irva, we are about the same size. I believe your dresses would fit me."

Irva looked at her, uncomprehending.

"That gray dress of yours with the matching bonnet, get it for me, please. The bonnet as well."

Irva continued to stare at her.

"Hurry! If I am away from the great hall much longer, Sir Rolf will send for me."

"But, miss . . ."

"Do as I say, Irva, and be quick about it!"

Irva rushed out of the apartment and down to the end of the hall to the room where her portmanteau had been left. She got the gray dress and bonnet and went back to Jocelyn, sure that the distraught young bride had taken leave of her senses. She watched silently as Jocelyn put on the dress and then carefully tucked her long black hair beneath the bonnet so that not a strand was visible.

"I shall try to explain to you as quickly as possible," Jocelyn said, "because I need your help. I am going to slip out of here and walk back to Egmont House . . ."

"Oh, Miss Jocelyn!" Irva wailed.

"It will take me most of the night, probably. In the morning I shall send Gerard back to get you and my luggage . . ."

"He will come in the morning, all right, but it will be to bring you back," Irva said.

"No, Irva. He said to me before he left that I have fulfilled our part of the contract. You see, the contract stated only that I was to marry Sir Rolf, which I did. It said nothing whatever about my living with him. So if I can get away now without being observed and get back to

Egmont House, there is nothing Sir Rolf can do. No power on earth can force me to live with him."

"Miss Jocelyn, you cannot possibly walk back to Egmont House!" Irva's eyes were round and shocked at the horrors which were going through her mind. "Think of the dangers! Why, it would not be safe during daylight, but at night . . . Oh, my Lord, you might even be kidnaped by highwaymen!"

"That would be preferable to remaining here," Jocelyn said calmly. "Do not be such a worrier, Irva. The plan will work, I assure you."

She tied the bonnet and turned to her abigail. "Now then, are you ready? What I want you to do is to go out ahead of me. Find the nearest and most deserted way for me to get to the woods behind Caradoc Court. I can go through the woods for a way, and then circle back toward the highway . . ."

"Miss Jocelyn, please . . ."

"Not another word, Irva. Nothing you can do or say can stop me now."

Irva nodded and listened to the remainder of the instructions Jocelyn gave her.

"As soon as I have gone, you are to come back here. I am sure it will not be long before Sir Rolf sends for me. You are to say that I shall be along directly. Eventually, he probably will come himself, and then you are to say that I just left and that, as far as you know, I was going to rejoin him in the great hall. He will think that I went the opposite way from the way he came, so he will most likely go back to the hall." She gave a mirthless little laugh. "Under different circumstances, this could be a game I enjoyed. The point is, Irva, you must stall him as long as you can to give me more time to get away. And you are, by no means, to let him know where I have gone. Say that you do not know, say anything, but do not let him send anyone along the highway looking for me. Do you understand?"

"Yes, miss."

"Good, then let us be on our way. As I said, you go first to be sure no one is in sight."

Irva embraced Jocelyn briefly and Jocelyn thought she saw tears glistening in her abigail's eyes, but she pushed her away from her, saying, "Now, now, none of that. We do not have time to get emotional. Besides, it will all turn out well, you will see."

Irva nodded, unable to speak. She opened the door, looked down the hall in both directions, then motioned for Jocelyn to follow her. At the end of the wing where the hall turned to the adjoining wing, Irva pointed to a short stairway and door which led to the outside. Jocelyn waited until Irva had opened the door and peered out, and then she went outside herself and looked straight toward the forest.

"All right, I shall leave you here," she whispered. "If anyone sees me crossing to the woods, they will not have the least notion who I am. And remember, Irva, I shall send Gerard for you tomorrow. He can tell Sir Rolf where I am then." She smiled a little at the thought of Gerard's discomfiture. But there was nothing that Sir Rolf could do to get her back, nor could he call Gerard out now. The contract had been met to the letter, if not the spirit.

Jocelyn patted Irva's shoulder, whispered, "Good-by for now," and hurried across the clearing to the woods.

The sun was still high in the sky, but she knew she did not have too many hours before dark, and she would have to be out of the woods and on the highway by sunset, otherwise she might get hopelessly lost and have to spend the night in the dark forest. That prospect left her feeling very unsure of herself and caused her bravado, most of which had been forced for Irva's benefit, to vanish entirely.

She walked faster and as she reached the edge of the woods, she looked back. There was no one in sight except Irva still standing in the doorway. She waved and motioned to Irva to go back inside. Then she went into the forest which was so thick with trees that it seemed that night had already fallen. Gingerly, she put one foot in front of the other, almost on tiptoe as though she were afraid of disturbing someone's slumber. The farther into the woods she went, the darker it became.

Her fear of getting lost and having to spend the night in the forest increased. But nothing—she comforted herself with the thought—could be worse than having to spend the night in that terrible house with that terrible man . . . her husband.

Five

Jocelyn had never been frightened before, so the feeling was new to her. She had grown up in a home with loving parents, a brother with whom she had been congenial if not close, and devoted servants. Fear was as foreign to her nature as was the sense of danger which now engulfed her.

She stopped perfectly still and looked around her in the darkening woods. There were strange noises which made her wonder what sort of wild animals lurked behind or in the trees ready to pounce upon her. Even some of the bird calls she heard were completely different from any she had ever heard before, and here in the woods they had an eerie quality. These were things she had not considered when she made her plans to escape from Caradoc Court.

Also, from the house, the forest had appeared much smaller than it did now that she was actually in it. For a moment she wondered if she should give up her plan and go back to the house, but then the thought of Sir Rolf waiting for her in the great hall, licking his lips as though in anticipation of devouring some delectable morsel, caused her to start walking again deeper into the dark green unknown. Anything was better than spending a lifetime married to a man she abhorred and living with him in a house so grotesque that merely walking down a hallway could make her blood run cold. And then there was Edward, the brother, to be considered. It was obvious from the way he looked at her that he neither liked nor approved of her. If she stayed at Caradoc Court, she would have only one friend: Irva.

She pushed on through the woods, quickening her pace, pushing at weeds and underbrush with both hands and feet. It seemed apparent that no one ever came into the woods for any reason or there would have been some sort of pathway or trail; therefore, her logic told her, if she could manage to carry out her original plan of circling slowly westward and staying in the woods until she came out at the highway, she would be safe. No one would think to look for her in the woods. But progress was much slower than she had expected because of the density of the growth. And she had to remember to be very careful in judging time, as well as the amount of curving from her point of entry, or else she would have no idea where she was when she emerged. For that matter, if she was not exceedingly careful about direction, she might not come out at all. It would be possible to become hopelessly lost as in a jungle, and to keep circling around the same area.

Do not panic, she kept telling herself. Keep a cool head. Forget the strange noises and strange animals. After all, she had never heard of man-eating animals in Buckinghamshire.

This thought gave her the courage to walk a little faster, although she was now in some pain from the scratches on her hands. She had forgotten gloves, and the brambles she pushed aside had torn the skin in several places. But she could not let this deter her. Whenever she began to lag a little in her walk, she thought of Sir Rolf, and that thought gave her the strength to continue at a fair pace.

She was aware, finally, of being almost overcome by exhaustion, and at the same time she realized that the gradually fading light was almost entirely gone. Night was settling over the countryside, and the woods, which had been dark in the beginning, were now becoming black.

There was no longer any need to rush to try to get out of the forest before day ended, for the night had settled in and a stillness far more frightening than the rustling noises caused her to catch her breath and, for a short while, to stand trembling as she strained her eyes trying to see through the blackness. When a shrill birdcall sounded nearby, she started violently, wondering if the bird were angry at her intrusion into his territory. She leaned against the trunk of a large tree to rest while she tried to decide which way and how much to change her direction.

Her dress, the dress she had borrowed from Irva, was torn in several places at the bottom where it had caught on briars as well as roots protruding from the ground. For the first time, it occurred to her that when she reached the highway she would look completely bedraggled, and thus might attract unwanted attention during her long walk home. She would have to remember, whenever she heard a horseman or carriage approaching, to get far enough off the highway so she would not be noticed.

The highway, she thought. Here she was wasting time thinking about what to do when she reached the road, when the main thing now was just to get out of the woods.

Some of her spirit returned and she began walking again, trudging along slowly and carefully, but with a strong will to succeed. She was sure that once she got to Egmont House everything would be all right. Gerard would take her in without anger, she was sure, because when he had told her good-by he had taken her hand

and held it briefly, and the look he had given her had been like an apology. He might be a little dismayed at seeing her, but in the long run, all would be well. Was that not what he had said to her? *You have kept our part of the contract, and all is well.*

Soon she would be back in her beloved Egmont House. Soon she could bathe her tired body, put a soothing balm on her scratches, lie down in her own bed, and sleep and sleep. When she awoke, all of this would be like a bad dream which had vanished with the sunrise of a new day.

These were the thoughts which kept her trudging on, tripping several times, and falling to the ground twice, but getting up each time, and going on without a moment's hesitation.

Then, suddenly, she stopped, realizing that something was terribly wrong. If she had been going in the right direction, angling her path ever slightly to the left, she should have reached the highway by now. It was obvious to her that she was nowhere near the road, nor even close to a clearing of any kind. She was still deep in the woods and for all she knew she could have slowly circled back toward Caradoc Court. If she came out near the house, she probably would not recognize it, for she had never seen the house at night, indeed, had scarcely looked at the outside during the day. Sir Rolf might have servants out looking for her and she could visualize herself being captured and taken before him like an escaped prisoner.

Again, fear rose in her, growing to near panic. She felt tears begin to slide down her cheeks, but she quickly brushed them away. It would do no good to cry; it would only take energy that she needed for completing her escape.

For the first time, she was aware of her physical discomfort. Not only were her scratches stinging, but she was cold, freezing cold. The dampness of the chilly night had penetrated to her bones, and she was shivering.

Hardly aware of what she was doing, she sat down on the ground. There was no point in going on. She was hopelessly lost and she might as well admit it.

But she was not ready yet to admit failure in her plan. No, she would never go back to Caradoc Court! The only thing she could do now was to wait until the morning light came through the trees to show her the way out of the forest.

Tired to the bone, she lay down, using her right arm to cushion her head and to keep her face from touching soft, damp moss which she imagined to be crawling with tiny insects. Almost immediately, she fell asleep.

She did not know how long she slept, but she was aware suddenly of sitting up in an attitude of listening. Some noise, not of the forest, had awakened her. She listened intently, but all was quiet now. As she was about to lie back down, she heard brush being broken, twigs snapping as though under unusually heavy footsteps, and then she heard the soft whinny of a horse.

She jumped up, her first sensation one of terror. Obviously, she was closer to the highway than she had thought and a night rider had taken a shortcut through the woods, going to the highway from the road on the other side of Caradoc Court. What if she were found here, a lone woman in the middle of the night?

Then her racing heart calmed some as more practical thoughts came into her head. The night rider could turn out to be a marvelous piece of luck for her. She could follow behind the horse—at a distance great enough so she would not be heard and discovered—and the horseman could lead her right out of the forest and to the highway. By morning she could be well on her way to Egmont House.

She heard the horse coming nearer and then, through the trees, she glimpsed a light, a lantern hanging from the side of the saddle. She realized the horse was headed straight toward the tiny clearing where she was standing, so she backed quickly into the nearest thicket of bushes. As she did, the branch of a bush broke off with a loud snap.

The horse, reaching the clearing at that point, turned his head, gave a loud snort, and reared suddenly, unseating his rider and causing him to slide off the back of the saddle and hit the ground with a loud thump. He lay deathly still, his left leg twisted beneath him. The lantern, still burning, fell beside his head.

The horse, calmer now, turned around and surveyed the scene as though wondering what had happened.

Jocelyn, her blood congealing, also looked at the scene, one thought only in her mind: she had been the cause of the horse's fright, the cause of the rider's death. She who had worried about being murdered in the woods had turned out to be the murderer.

But then the man on the ground moved slightly and groaned. She left the thicket of bushes and approached him saying, "Please, sir, I did not mean to frighten your horse. It was entirely unintentional. What can I do to help you?"

He groaned again and she thought: What if his leg is broken and he cannot move? How will I ever get help to come here when I have no notion where we are?

She was beside the man now, and as he raised up on one elbow, she recognized him in the lanternlight and, involuntarily, she screamed. It was Sir Rolf. The man she had caused to be thrown to the ground was her new husband.

He recognized her in the same moment that she recognized him, and the expression on his face changed from one of pure pain to one that included disgust as well.

He drew in a long breath and said, "So! It was you who caused my horse to rear, you instead of a wild animal!"

She watched him as he tried to get up, failed, and sank back to the ground with a loud groan.

"Help!" she called, "Oh, someone help us!" She could not tell how badly he was injured or whether his leg was broken, but if he had been out looking for her, certainly there must be others nearby, a search party.

He raised his hand, silencing her. "Hush, madam, there is no one to hear you. Do you think I wanted even a servant to know that my wife abandoned me as soon as the ceremony was over?"

"Then what are we to do?" Her only thought right now was what to do for the injured man. The fact that she was the cause of his injury took precedence over the thought that he had found her.

He tried again to move, a low moan and a curse escaping his lips simultaneously. "I do not think the leg is broken but, damme, it does pain me—and my back as well. Were you trying to kill me, madam? Murder me in cold blood?"

"Of course not!" she gasped. "I did not even know it was you until you were on the ground and I saw your face in the lanternlight. Oh, I did not mean to frighten your horse or cause you injury. You must believe me."

"Then what, may I inquire, were you doing here in the forest in the middle of the night? Surely you did not think I would mistake your actions for those of a loving bride?"

She could not tell from his tone of voice which was greater, his pain or his anger, but she was well aware that, had he been able to move about freely, he probably would have struck her with all his strength. Therefore, she kept her distance from him, but now she realized that the only way to get him to where they could obtain help was for her to get him back onto his horse. She took a step toward him and asked, "Do you think you could remount with my help? I could lead your horse and . . ."

"God's nightshirt, woman! First you try to kill me and, failing that, you try to get me lost in the woods as you apparently are." With a mighty effort, he managed to sit up. "Here, take the lantern over to that tree. Do you see where I mean? Now, shine it on the other side of the tree. Do you see a path there, a small path leading out from the clearing?"

She looked down at the ground. Yes, there was a path. She could see it now in the light, but without the light, she would never have known it was there.

"All right," he said, "with the lantern, follow that path. It will lead you to a cottage about half a mile from here. Tell the woman who lives in the cottage that I have had a fall and cannot get back on my horse. Tell her to come back here with you."

"Shall I bring anything else?" she asked, wondering about medicine or something with which to make a splint for his leg.

"Just the woman," he said, his voice low and guttural as he growled the command. "Begone now, and do not take the rest of the night in returning!"

Jocelyn held the lantern in front of her and hurried along the path as fast as she dared, but even with the light she stumbled occasionally in her haste. Cold chills went up her spine, but she did not know whether they were caused by the chill of the night or by dread of whatever would happen to her now. If Sir Rolf had been so embarrassed by her leaving that he had not even told a servant, it was clear to her that he would never forgive her for the humiliation as well as the pain she was causing him. For it would be obvious to everyone what had happened as soon as they returned to Caradoc Court. There was no way to explain her bedraggled appearance or his middle-of-the-night ride through the forest or his injury. One look at them would tell the whole story. And, although she did not know her new husband very well, she sensed that humiliation would not be borne by him under any circumstances. What would he do to her? Would he lock her in her room to keep her from trying to escape again? Would he beat her as though she were a recalcitrant puppy he was trying to train? She knew instinctively that he would not be above giving her either punishment, or any other that might come into his mind.

That being the way the matter stood, why did she not just go on with the lantern, leave him there all night? The path surely went beyond the cottage he told her about and on through the woods to the highway. There was no question but that he would be found in the morning and taken care of, and by that time she could be well on her way back home.

No, she could not do that. She could not leave him lying there, not knowing how badly he was injured or whether he would be found. She would have to return with help for she had been the cause of his needing that help.

The cottage loomed suddenly in front of her, its thatched roof standing out like a bonnet on a small head. All was dark within and she wondered suddenly who else lived there besides the woman Sir Rolf had mentioned. The thought of having to explain their predicament to several strangers gave her a better understanding of Sir Rolf's humiliation over his wife's deserting him.

She knocked at the door, timidly at first, and waited. When there was no sound, she knocked louder and louder, and finally called, "Is anyone in there? Please open the door. I need help."

Suddenly a woman's voice startled her, coming through the window beside the door, "Who's out there? What is it?"

"Please," Jocelyn said again, "I need help. Sir Rolf has fallen from his horse a short distance from here and he has been hurt. He asked me to come for you and to bring you back to where he is."

"And just who might you be, out in the woods in the middle of the night?" It was obvious the woman inside suspected some trick. Perhaps she thought if she opened the door, robbers would step out of the shadows and into the house.

"I am . . ." Jocelyn hesitated. Even under the circumstances she could hardly bring herself to say the word. "I am his wife," she said finally.

There was a long silence, followed by a mirthless laugh from within the house and then the door was thrown open and a woman in a nightdress appeared in the light of the lantern. "Well, that does beat all!" she said, a trace of laughter still in her voice. "So you are his new bride. A babe in the woods!" This time her laughter gave signs of continuing through the night, but finally she stopped. "Fell off his horse, did he? No better than he deserves, if you ask me."

"Will you come with me, please?" Jocelyn did not understand or care what the woman found so amusing if only she could get her to go back to Sir Rolf with her. "He said for you to come . . ."

"Oh, I am sure of that. Just be a minute while I find my cloak." The woman disappeared inside the house and returned shortly with a long navy cloak thrown over her nightdress and a lantern in her right hand. "Thought we might need some more light," she said.

Jocelyn had not been able to see the woman clearly before, but now she got a good look at her. She was thin and wiry, a middle-aged woman with graying hair and thick eyebrows which almost hid her eyes.

"Do you . . . live back there?" Jocelyn asked as they made their way along the path.

"Of course I live there," the woman said gruffly. "Why else would I be sleeping there? I am the seamstress for Caradoc Court. I gather Sir Rolf has not told you about me yet."

"No, I suppose there had not been time . . ."

"I do all the sewing," the woman said, "and sometimes I help out in other ways when needed. Like tonight." Her thin laugh had a bitter sound. "My name is Maeve Mc-Caulay."

"We are nearly there . . . to the place," Jocelyn said, thinking she heard a noise which sounded like a horse pawing at the ground. "Yes, here we are."

They went out into the tiny clearing and there was Sir Rolf, exactly as Jocelyn had left him. The horse, still standing nearby, whinnied as they approached.

"You took your own sweet time," Sir Rolf sputtered at Jocelyn. "I daresay you were in no hurry. Maeve, I want none of your tongue tonight. The two of you are to get me on my horse and back to your cottage."

"Why, sire," Maeve said with false sweetness, "I cannot for the life of me think how you came to be in these straits. But I shall take you to my cottage forthwith, and my home shall be your home for the night." The woman stood behind Sir Rolf, placed her arms around his chest and tugged at him, pulling him to his feet. Jocelyn watched, amazed at her strength.

Sir Rolf began groaning and cursing. "What are you trying to do, woman?" he thundered. "Are you both intent upon seeing me dead? Damme, my life is suddenly filled with nothing but perverse women." Then he broke off and screamed out in pain as Maeve and Jocelyn tried to get him upon the horse. It took a long time, plus all of their combined strength, for although Sir Rolf could stand on one leg, his other leg was utterly useless, and he cried out in pain at the least jarring of his back. Finally, though, with Sir Rolf holding on to the saddle, and Maeve bearing the rest of his weight, Jocelyn managed to get his good leg into the stirrup and then he was able to swing over onto the horse.

Sir Rolf heaved a deep sigh and let the upper part of his body fall over the mane of the horse. "Walk the horse slowly, very slowly," he said.

Maeve let Jocelyn carry the two lanterns ahead in the path and she followed, leading the horse, apparently unmindful of the reproaches Sir Rolf was heaping upon her, but mostly upon Jocelyn, calling her "ungrateful wench," "mercenary cheat," and other names to which Jocelyn finally closed her ears. Again, she found tears falling, but she knew this time it was mostly from fatigue, for she discovered suddenly that she was so tired she could hardly put one foot in front of the other. She did not care what Sir Rolf called her or what he thought. All she wanted was to lie down and never get up again.

When they reached the cottage, Maeve tied the horse's reins to the trellis over the door, then she and Jocelyn had to go through the almost impossible process of getting Sir Rolf off the horse. When he was down, it was Maeve who put her arm around him and helped him into the house. Jocelyn could not have borne to touch him again.

Jocelyn watched at the bedroom door while Maeve laid him gently across the bed. When she began removing his shoes, Jocelyn turned away.

"You'll have to sleep in the room with me, m'lady," Maeve called to her.

Jocelyn was too tired to answer. Taking a lantern, she went through the small house until she found the other bedroom, and, without removing any of her clothes, she fell into bed. The last thing she heard before she slipped into unconsciousness was Sir Rolf crying out in pain, and then shouting to her, "As soon as daylight comes, I shall send for the carriage to take us back to Caradoc Court. Then we shall see what will happen to you, my pretty, murderous bride!"

Six

The first pink rays of dawn had just crossed the sky when Edward was awakened by a servant. He sat up in bed and looked blankly around the room, for he still was not quite accustomed to his new quarters in the servants' wing of the house.

"What is it?" he asked, knowing immediately that something was wrong.

It was Rolf's valet, John, who had awakened him. The man appeared quite agitated. "It's the woman from the cottage, sir, that Mrs. McCaulay. She's here saying that Sir Rolf and his wife are at her cottage and that Sir Rolf has had an accident. He wants you to bring the carriage to the cottage to get him."

"What kind of accident?" Edward was out of bed at once. "Are they hurt?" He knew nothing of what had happened yesterday, for as soon as Rolf dismissed him from the wedding breakfast, he had ridden into the village to visit with friends, and had allowed them to persuade him to stay for supper. He had not returned to Caradoc Court until late in the evening. Since he no longer shared the wing of the house with Rolf, he had no idea but that the master of Caradoc Court and his wife were in the apartment Rolf had fixed up to be the bridal chamber.

What in thunder were they doing at Maeve McCaulay's, and at this ungodly hour of the morning?

He would find out in good time, he supposed. He rushed to put on his clothes, telling John to see that the carriage was in the courtyard at once. "And be prepared to go with me," Edward added. "You may be needed."

"No, sir," John said. "That Mrs. McCaulay said you were to come alone."

Edward could not even begin to imagine what had happened to his brother and his brother's bride. They obviously had not been out for an early morning ride, because the carriage was here, and he doubted seriously if they had ridden out on horses, because Rolf was not overly fond of horses and only rode when absolutely necessary. And the most puzzling question of all: Why were they out so early the morning after their wedding day?

He went out into the courtyard, jumped into the carriage and took the reins from John, who got out immediately. Cracking the reins over the pair's backs, he started out as fast as he deemed it safe to go on the rocky, seldom used road which led to the part of the forest where the McCaulay cottage was situated.

When he reached the edge of the forest, he halted the pair of grays and then proceeded at a snail's pace along the narrow path to the cottage. He was not even sure the carriage could make it safely. Finally, though, he was in sight of the cottage, and as he drew closer, he saw the McCaulay woman standing in front, peering down the path as though eager for him to arrive.

"What has happened?" he said as soon as he jumped down. "I understand there has been an accident."

The woman pulled her shawl tighter about her and nodded. "*She* says it was an accident, but he says it was intentional. Could be she was trying to do him in."

"What in the name of heaven are you talking about?" Edward could make no sense whatever of her words.

Then she told him about Jocelyn coming to her door in the middle of the night and of the two of them going back to get Sir Rolf. "They stayed the rest of the night here," she said, "though the good Lord knows we none of us got any sleep. Except *her*, and as far as I know, she is still asleep. And he carried on all night, moaning and groaning, and saying he wouldn't be in this fix but for her, and that she had wanted to do him in, and that she nearly got what she wanted, but he would see she never got anything she wanted again, and so on and on. So anxious to get rid of them I am that I went to Caradoc Court before first light to leave word for you to come with the carriage."

Still unable to sort out the facts in his mind and decide what last night's escapade had been about, Edward went inside the house. "Where are they?" he asked, and Maeve led the way to the bedroom where Sir Rolf, dozing lightly, lay on his side, a pillow under his left leg and another at his back. He opened his eyes while Edward looked down at him.

"Damme!" he cried, "you took the devil's own time getting here. I could have breathed my last while you were dallying along."

"I came as soon as I knew you were here," Edward said calmly, realizing that his brother was in no immediate danger of facing his Maker, but seeing that he was in a good deal of pain. "I should have brought the doctor with me," he added.

"No! Never!" Sir Rolf was becoming mysteriously riled, Edward thought. "You get me out of here and back to Caradoc Court, *then* you can send for the doctor. And right now, man, there's not a minute to lose."

Edward nodded to Maeve, and the two of them managed to get Sir Rolf out of bed and to the carriage. It took longer, however, to get him into the carriage, and he was cursing and groaning with every breath he took. Finally, settled in the seat, he looked at Maeve and nodded. "You did what you could," he said, his way of thanking her.

"You are forgetting something, aren't you?" Maeve asked in a sarcastically sweet tone of voice.

"What is that?"

"Your wife, sire. Or did you expect to leave her here with me?"

"That ungrateful wench!" Sir Rolf bellowed. "Go and get her, Edward."

"Where is she?" Edward asked Maeve.

"The other bedroom. She was still asleep last time I looked in on her."

Edward went back into the house. The door to the bedroom was partially open, but the shutters were closed and it was dark inside so he could see nothing. He knocked lightly at the door and when there was no response, he pushed the door open and went in. He went to the window and opened the shutters, letting the still rising sun in, and then he looked at the bed.

Jocelyn, apparently in a deep sleep, lay on top of the coverlet, fully clothed. A light blanket had been thrown across her from the waist down, and he assumed Maeve had done it. Her hands, on top of the blanket, were full of scratches and dried blood, and her face was smudged with dirt. She was indeed a pitiful sight to behold, but Edward's curiosity was greater than his pity. Why had she and Rolf been out in the woods in the middle of the night, their wedding night at that? Why had he been on horseback but she on foot?

Could she have run away? he wondered, then immediately put that thought out of his mind. Never would one so eager to be mistress of Caradoc Court have run away. But why was Rolf so angry with her? Why did he keep blaming her for his accident?

Edward knew that his chances for learning the whole story were not very great, for it was doubtful if the girl would tell him, and even more doubtful if Rolf would tell him the truth about the affair.

He almost hated to awaken Jocelyn for she looked like a sick young animal who had been in a terrible fight. For a moment, looking at her face, he felt sorry for her because she looked so young and defenseless . . . and so miserable, even in sleep.

Then, remembering that she was a mercenary schemer and not the young innocent she appeared to be, he came to the conclusion that she deserved whatever she had got . . . and would get later.

He put his hand on her shoulder and roughly shook her awake.

Jocelyn sat up with a start, a scream almost escaping from her lips before she realized that she was not being harmed. She looked around the strange room, recalling slowly the terrible events of the preceding day and night, and then she looked at . . . Edward. His dark head was inclined and a scowl was on his face. "The carriage from Caradoc Court is outside," he said. "We are waiting for you."

She threw back the blanket and arose slowly and stiffly, almost falling as she tried to stand. Edward grasped her arm and steadied her. "I thought it was only my brother who was injured," he said. "Are you hurt also?"

"No," she said, "I am quite all right." Those words, she thought, were laughable, but she did not feel like laughing. Indeed, she doubted that she would ever feel all right or like laughing again.

When she tried to walk across the room, she found her feet were so sore that each step was torture. Again, Edward took her arm and this time held onto it until he had helped her in the carriage.

"Thank you for all you did for us," Jocelyn said to Maeve, who was still standing by the carriage waiting for her uninvited guests to depart. "I do not know how we would have managed without you," Jocelyn added.

Maeve shrugged and made no answer. She went back into the cottage as soon as Edward took up the reins. It was obvious that she was relieved to be rid of her troublesome and troubled company.

The ride to Caradoc Court was not long, but to Jocelyn it seemed an eternity. None of them spoke a word, and the only sounds were the horses' hooves on the ground and Sir Rolf's moans with every turn of the carriage wheels.

John was waiting when the carriage arrived in the courtyard and he and Edward took the injured man inside. Jocelyn followed, not knowing what else to do.

"Where are you taking me," Sir Rolf roared when they passed the door to the apartment where Jocelyn had stayed.

"To your old room," Edward said. "I did not suppose you felt up to sharing a room . . . just yet."

Sir Rolf said nothing else and the three men disappeared into a room further down the hall while Jocelyn stood uncertainly before the door to the apartment.

"Oh, miss, just look at you!" The door opened suddenly, and there was Irva, her concern showing plainly in her face.

"Irva!" Jocelyn flung herself into her abigail's arms and the tears she had tried so hard to hold back for the past hours finally spilled over, building up into great sobs.

Irva led her into the small sitting room, murmuring,

"There, there," as she sat her down. "We'll just take these dirty, torn clothes off of you and get you into a warm bath. Oh, Miss Jocelyn, whatever have you done to your hands?"

But Jocelyn was still too upset to answer. All she wanted now was the bath Irva had mentioned, some clean clothing and . . . some food. She was suddenly ravenously hungry and she realized she had not eaten for nearly twenty-four hours.

The sound of voices in the hall an hour or so later caused Jocelyn to look up from the tray of food which Irva had had a maidservant bring from the kitchen. She had had her bath and Irva had put a soothing lotion over her scratched hands. Now, in a new dress—part of her hastily made trousseau—she was beginning to feel a little more like the old Jocelyn. For the first time since entering the apartment with Irva, she thought of her husband down the hall and wondered if the doctor had arrived and relieved his pain. She recognized Edward's voice in the hall, but the other was that of a stranger. She went to the door.

Edward and an older man were walking down the hall toward the door to the courtyard. They both turned and looked at her.

"Madam," Edward said, and the iciness of his tone sent a shiver through her, "may I present Dr. Griswold to you?" And to the doctor: "My sister-in-law, Rolf's wife." Turning to Jocelyn again, he continued, "Dr. Griswold has just seen Rolf, and I am happy to report that his injuries are not as serious as I had thought."

"There are no broken bones," the doctor said, "neither back nor leg, though they both appear to be badly strained. He will have to remain in bed for about a month in order to effect a complete cure."

Jocelyn breathed a sigh of relief, then asked a question which had been bothering her. "He will not be . . . crippled, will he?"

"Not unless he tries to become too active before the strain is gone," the doctor said. "He also has some bad-looking bruises, but they will go away in time."

"I am glad of that," she said, much relieved to know that the injuries she had caused would not be permanent.

"My brother would like to see you in his room," Edward said.

"Now?" she asked.

"At your earliest convenience," Edward said, and he and the doctor continued down the hall and went outside.

Jocelyn went to the door of Sir Rolf's room and stood hesitantly before it, knowing she had to go in, yet dreading the ordeal so much that her hand began to shake as she raised it to knock.

"Come!" Sir Rolf shouted in answer to the rap.

She went in and closed the door, then leaned against it, wanting to get no closer to the man propped up in bed by at least half a dozen pillows.

"Well, madam," he said immediately, "I trust you are satisfied, seeing the havoc you have wreaked!"

"I am truly sorry about your injuries," she said, "but I am glad they are not so serious."

"Not serious! Egad, woman, I am to be bedridden for a month or more, and you say my injuries are not serious!" His voice became louder and louder, and she wondered if he ever, at any time, spoke in well-modulated tones or if shouting was just second-nature with him.

"What I meant was that I am glad you received no permanent damage." She was determined not to let him either rile or frighten her. Her spirit was returning, and she decided that now was as good a time as any to have it out with him.

"It is no thanks to you that I am alive," he said.

"We are in agreement, then, that I have brought you bad luck, therefore, I am sure you will not be sorry to learn that I plan to leave here as soon as I can get word to my brother to come for me . . . unless, of course, you would consider sending me back to Egmont House in your carriage."

He looked at her for a long time as though he had understood nothing she had said. Then he said, wonder in his voice, "You have gone completely mad. Tell me— if you know—what is the meaning of what you are saying."

Gaining confidence, she went to the side of the bed and sat down in a large chair. "It was wrong of me to run away from here before I had time to think out what I was doing. I should simply have sent word to my brother yesterday, perhaps a messenger could have caught him before he got back to Egmont House . . ."

"What are you saying?" Sir Rolf cried. He tried to raise himself to an upright position, cringed with pain, then fell back to the pillows. "You are making no sense whatever. Has it not penetrated your brain, assuming that you have one, that you are now married to me and that you cannot go running back to Egmont House. Caradoc Court is your home now."

"I am aware, sir," she said slowly, "of the marriage contract my brother signed. The agreement was that I marry you, which I have done. There was nothing in the contract that stated I had to live with you. Now that I have fulfilled my part of the agreement, I consider myself free to leave."

Sir Rolf was looking at her in astonishment, and then he began to laugh, an unpleasant noise that sounded like the rumble of distant thunder. Then he choked on his laughter and stopped abruptly. "Excuse me, my dear, but I had a picture of your brother's face were you suddenly to appear at your old home again." There was another short, menacing chuckle. "Apparently you do not know as much as you think you do about your brother's bargain—though God knows *you* have not turned out to be a bargain. Perhaps I had better explain to you the terms of the contract. You see, my pretty, although I gave your brother a check to be cashed after our wedding, it was not for a very large amount. The agreement states that he is to receive an allowance every month for himself and for the upkeep of Egmont House."

Jocelyn gasped as the full meaning of this struck her.

"Yes, my dear wife, the day you leave me is the day the money stops." Sir Rolf had a wide smile on his face as he added, "And I do not imagine that your money-hungry brother is going to let you go home, probably not even for a short visit."

Jocelyn stared down at the floor, all hope gone. She knew as well as Sir Rolf—better than Sir Rolf—what Gerard's reaction would be to her sudden appearance at Egmont House and her announcement that she had left her husband. He would take her back to Caradoc Court so fast that she would not even have time to catch her breath.

"You are my wife, and nothing can change that," Sir Rolf said. "So you would do well to keep this fact in mind and act accordingly."

She looked up at the triumphant expression on his face and knew that she despised him, totally and completely and for all time. Unable to say a word, she got up quickly and left the room.

Edward, having seen Dr. Griswold off, was on his way back to Rolf's room when he saw the door open and Jocelyn come out. She stopped in the middle of the hall and put her hands over her face. He could not tell whether she was crying, but he could imagine that she might well be. Rolf had had no hesitancy in saying—*continually!*—that it was Jocelyn who had caused his accident. Regardless of what had led to the accident, Edward could not help but feel a little sorry for the stricken-looking girl at this instant. There was no doubt but that she had just undergone her first experience with Rolf's terrible temper. What she had seen of it probably had been only a preamble.

He went to her. "Madam, er . . . I mean . . ." It occurred to him that he did not know what to call her. He did not know her well enough, nor did he want, to use the familiarity of her first name, and he would feel foolish addressing his brother's wife as Lady Caradoc.

She started and took her hands away from her face when he spoke. "You may call me Jocelyn," she said, as though reading his thoughts, adding with bitterness, "Since we shall probably see each other every day for the rest of our lives, I see no need to stand on formality."

"I gather the prospect is less than pleasing to you," Edward commented. "Truthfully, I cannot remember ever seeing a more unhappy-looking bride."

"And it is unlikely you ever shall," she said, starting toward her own door.

He opened the door for her and followed her into the little sitting room. "I have no idea how you and Rolf came to be in the woods last night or whether he is speaking truthfully when he says that you caused his accident, but I do want to say that I can sympathize with you on the scene you have just been through with him. I know his temper well and . . ."

"I will tell you how I came to be in the woods," she interrupted. "I was running away from here. I was trying to get to the highway so I could go home."

"Running away!" He did not believe a word of it. It

made no sense at all for her to run away just after she
had succeeded in getting what she wanted.

"Yes, I was running away," she repeated. "Your brother
did not want anyone to know his bride had deserted him,
so he did not even let the servants know. He went looking
for me himself on his horse, and he found me in the
woods in the middle of the night. The McCaulay woman
told you the rest."

Although her gaze through those blue-gray eyes was
steady, Edward could not believe a word she was saying.
It would only make an already unpleasant situation more
unpleasant for him to call her a liar, however, so what he
said to her was: "You are not a very loyal wife to tell
something your husband does not want known."

"It makes no difference to me who knows it," she said,
"no difference at all."

She was, he decided, as hard as nails in spite of the
outward innocent look of her. When it was so obvious
that his brother had bought her—and at how dear a
price?—how could she expect anyone to believe this little
act she was putting on now, this pretense that she would
rather be at her former home than here. It stood to reason
that if she had sold out virtue, honor, and all the other
values of gentlefolk in order to be the mistress of Caradoc
Court, she most assuredly would not run away before she
had enjoyed the fruits of her misdeeds. He returned her
steady gaze and said, "Perhaps you will be good enough
to explain to me why if you wanted to marry Rolf, you
suddenly wanted to leave before you had spent so much
as a night here."

"You think I wanted to . . ." Her eyes now flashed
indignantly. "You think I . . ." She appeared too angry
to continue.

"I saw no one forcing you to come here today," he
said. "You entered the chapel willingly, on the arm of

your brother, and clad in a wedding dress which was obviously made for you."

She pointed to the door. "Will you be so good as to leave?"

He could only stare at her, surprised at her outburst. "Please go!"

Her abigail walked into the room at that moment, so he left.

He started toward Rolf's door, then changed his mind. He had no desire to listen to any more of that one's outpourings today. Instead, he walked outside, going behind the house to the gardens.

Was it possible, he mused, that Rolf and Maeve had both been telling the truth when they said that Jocelyn had tried to murder Rolf? Could she possibly be that cold-blooded? He tried to picture in his mind what might have happened yesterday. Jocelyn, having become the mistress of Caradoc Court after the ceremony, might actually have plotted Rolf's death, not wanting to have to live with him as his wife. She could have pretended to run away, leaving clues so that Rolf would follow her into the woods. She could have known that he was not a good rider and deliberately have caused the horse to rear.

Then he saw her face in his mind, those calm eyes, the look of gentleness as well as gentility . . . Surely this girl could not have planned to kill his brother and then, coldly and calculatingly, carried out the plan. Surely the stricken look on her face when she came out of his room had not been because her plan had failed!

If he was doing her an injustice, a grave injustice at that, he was sorry. For if, indeed, *she* was the one who was telling the truth, then she had every right to her fury at him for so misjudging her.

All at once he was overcome by a feeling of . . . was it pity? . . . tenderness? . . . or concern? . . . for her.

He was also struck by an overwhelming feeling of confusion because he did not actually know what his sister-in-law was or what to think about her. If she was a mercenary, would-be murderer, then the thought of living in the same house with her was untenable. If, on the other hand, she was as she claimed, a victim, it made him unspeakably sad to think of her spending the rest of her life in this gloomy house, married to Rolf, a man she loathed.

After long thought, he decided he at least half believed her, for what had she to gain by marrying and then murdering Rolf, at least before she gave him an heir. If Rolf were to die now, the land, the title, everything would automatically go to Edward.

But did Jocelyn know this?

He was beginning to dislike himself and his state of mind. Not usually of a suspicious nature, it made him feel almost physically ill now to so distrust someone with whom he would be in close contact for a long time to come.

Yet it hurt him as much, made him feel equally ill, when he thought that Rolf might have been the one taking advantage of Jocelyn. But, all things considered, for the sake of keeping peace in the house, he had to try to believe Jocelyn. Knowing Rolf as he did, it would not be difficult.

Seven

Jocelyn slept much better than she had expected to the first night in her new home, and she awoke feeling much refreshed. Her spirits, however, were still low as she lay in bed remembering the events of yesterday and realizing, finally, that all avenues of escape were closed to her. Gerard would never allow her to return home, and, indeed, if she were to go somewhere else (though where else she could go, she had not the faintest notion) Gerard would be the first to join Sir Rolf in searching for her. Although she still cared about Gerard—she could not bring herself to despise her brother—she had no illusions about his motives, his bad points, or his virtues (though right now she could think of few virtues that he possessed). As bad as he was, however, Gerard with all his faults was far more appealing to her than her husband. She now detested Sir Rolf so thoroughly that she could not bear to be in his presence. The thought of spending her life here, married to him, made her almost physically ill. But there was no help for it now, so she decided she might as well accept her fate and bear it with as much good grace as she could muster.

With that thought in mind, she rose and prepared for her first full day at Caradoc Court.

After her breakfast, brought on a tray to her room by Irva, it occurred to her that she should know something about the house and that she should go from room to room to look over her new home. After all, if she was the mistress of Caradoc Court, she should at least see the vast house over which she ostensibly presided.

As she was getting ready to leave her rooms, she turned to Irva, thinking for the first time that her abigail must be as lonely here as she herself was.

"Irva, do you find it intolerable here?" she asked. "If so, I will not keep you. You may go back to Egmont House."

"What would I do there, miss, with you here?" Irva asked practically.

"I had not thought of that," Jocelyn admitted. "Then perhaps you would rather be with your family."

"No, miss, my brothers and sisters are so scattered around that it would be impossible even to visit them all within a year. Caradoc Court is not so bad for me as it is for you, I think, and my place is here with you," she said loyally.

"I do thank you," Jocelyn said. "I cannot think what I would do without you."

She went out into the hall, casting her eye in the direction of Sir Rolf's door. The door was closed and all was quiet. She did not go down to that end of the hall but began her tour with the rooms next to her own. She went into all of them, room after room, obviously unoccupied, and she marveled at the size of the house and also the bad taste with which it was furnished. The furniture, all made from a dark wood, was massive and forbidding in appearance. It added considerably to the gloom of the house and to the oppressive atmosphere.

She did not tarry in any of the rooms, for she found nothing that interested her—no *objet d'art*, no curtains or draperies or any other furnishings that lightened the motif of any room. Everywhere she looked all was dark and dreary. The gargoyles were the worst of all; they repelled her. She could not imagine why anyone would want those evil faces leering in every room.

She left the west wing and went to the north wing. The hall opened into the small dining room which she had not seen before. It could have been a charming room, she thought, but like all the others, it depressed her. Apparently the same bad taste prevailed throughout the house.

From the dining room she went into a huge, empty room, and she stood in the middle of the floor wondering why the room had never been furnished. Then it occurred to her that this was the ballroom, and she looked around, trying in vain to imagine the room filled with dancing, happy people. Conviviality in any form seemed totally foreign to Caradoc Court.

From the ballroom she went into the great hall, and after the first glance, she closed her eyes. She wished she never had to see this room again, for she would never be able to view it or even think of it without seeing in her mind the wedding breakfast: she and Sir Rolf sitting at the head of the tremendous table with Gerard and Edward on each side of them . . . and of the four, Sir Rolf was the only one who had shown signs of being even remotely happy. Gerard, though pleased at the bargain he had struck, had appeared, nevertheless, at least a little remorseful, and Edward . . . She had no idea why her new brother-in-law had been glum to the point of rudeness. He had acted as though her very presence in this house was an insult to him.

She stopped dead still in the middle of the room and opened her eyes. Of course! It had come to her, in that instant, exactly why Edward treated her as he did, why he did not want her here. She had been told that the reason Sir Rolf was so anxious to get a wife was so he could have an heir and thus keep Edward from inheriting the estate and title. Naturally Edward resented her! He thought, no doubt, that she had married his brother in order to be mistress of this gloomy, miserable, loveless house, in order to have her children grow up here and eventually own, not only the house, but all of Sir Rolf's land. And one of her children, the eldest son, would inherit the title.

She felt sick and overcome by anger. Just thinking that anyone could hold such an opinion of her, even a stranger, caused her to grow hot with fury. Now she also knew the reason for Edward's seeming rudeness the day he had brought the betrothal ring to Egmont House. How could he possibly have thought that she . . . that *any* girl, for that matter . . . would willingly allow herself to be bought by a promise of worldly goods and a title from his repulsive brother?

Or had Sir Rolf told Edward, or implied, that such was the case? It would not be beyond her husband to do such a thing, she was sure. Listening to his accusations against her after the accident, when he had stated flatly that she had been trying to do him in, was enough to tell her that no level was so low that he would not stoop to it.

Sir Rolf and Edward. These were the two men with whom she would spend the rest of her life, unless Edward decided to take up residence elsewhere, which was not likely since he took care of all the business and kept the accounts of Caradoc Court.

She left the great hall, going through the door which led to the east wing.

She saw almost at once that she was in the servants' part of the house. There were no apartments here, and the rooms were smaller, and all of the doors stood open excepting two. Curiously, she opened the first one. It was a bedroom, the same size as the other rooms, but something about it seemed different from the others. She took a step inside the door and looked around.

There was a large chair beside the bed, upholstered in velvet, and on the marble-top table was a silver pitcher. On the bureau top was a matched pair of silver brushes. A huge wardrobe stood partly open, revealing fashionable coats and breeches, and in the corner of the room was a bookcase which, she saw upon closer inspection, contained a number of fine leather-bound volumes of Shakespeare's works.

Although in the servants' part of the house, this very definitely was not the room of one of the household staff.

She backed out of the room, feeling that she was trespassing, an infidel intruding in a sanctum.

She was more hesitant about opening the second closed door, her hand gingerly touching the knob as though she expected to be burned. She pushed the door slowly inward, stepped inside and looked squarely into the eyes of her brother-in-law!

Edward was seated at a desk, a large book of accounts open in front of him. Jocelyn gasped in surprise, then covered her mouth with her hand.

Edward stood up immediately. "You wanted to see me?" he asked.

"No, I . . . I . . ." She floundered, not knowing what to say that would not sound as though she were prying into the privacy of everything and everybody on the estate.

Edward smiled at her and she could detect no malice in the smile, though she herself felt anything but warm toward him. However, it was she who was now intruding in his domain, and so it was she who owed the apology.

"I do beg your pardon," she said. "I did not mean to interrupt your work or disturb you in any way. I was looking over the house, trying to familiarize myself . . ."

"Do let me escort you." Edward came from behind the desk. "I should have thought to offer."

"Oh, no," she said, backing off. She wanted to see as little of him as possible. "I have already seen the house, all of it."

"Then I shall show you the gardens," Edward said, taking her arm. "They are quite the nicest part of the house anyway, colorful, cheerful, bright, not a bit like this old mausoleum."

She jerked her arm away. "Please do not trouble yourself," and then she added, almost under her breath, "or me."

Undisturbed, Edward took her arm again, holding it firmer this time, and steered her out into the hall. "We shall begin first with my apology to you," he said. "Yesterday I made a dreadful statement. I called you a disloyal wife, and I also made some insinuations by not believing that you were telling the truth when you said you ran away . . ."

"That you could even *dream* that anyone would marry your brother voluntarily exhibits a certain amount of dullness on your part, sir," she said spiritedly.

He gave her an odd look, then said, "I am in complete agreement with you, and I wish to make up for my stupidity now. Will you please accept my humblest apologies and let us be friends?"

She could not tell, since she knew him so slightly, whether he was being sincere, or merely paying her lip service. He seemed contrite enough, and yet she could not forget the position in which he had put her yesterday, the way he had made her feel.

"Had I but chatted with you for a while the day I took the ring to Egmont House, or even after the wedding the day before yesterday, I would have known that you could never comport yourself in any way except with the greatest propriety and decorum," he said.

Was his tone mocking? She could not be sure, yet he was looking at her as though he wanted her for a friend, and she found her attitude toward him thawing in spite of herself.

"I never wanted this marriage," she said. "You must believe that."

"Oh, I do," he said. "I find that very easy to believe." He smiled again, and again she wondered about his sincerity.

"Your marriage may be a farce," he went on, "but because of it, we are now related, and I would much prefer to get on with my sister-in-law than not. Come, Jocelyn, what do you say?"

This time he really did seem to be speaking honestly, but she could not entirely forgive him for the anger and hard feelings he had caused in her. However, what he said did make good sense: they were in-laws, would be living under the same roof, and it certainly would be better if they were not always at each other's throats. Outwardly, at least, she could be pleasant to him. Her real thoughts about him could be kept safely inside.

She gave him a half smile. "I think we can be friends, Mr. Caradoc," she said, keeping her reservations about such a friendship to herself.

"Edward," he said. "For heaven's sake, call me Edward."

"Edward," she repeated.

"Much better," he said. "Now then, we shall continue your tour. I think you will like the outside of Caradoc Court much better than the inside. I know I do."

They went first to the gardens behind the east wing of the house, and Jocelyn caught her breath at the loveliness displayed before her. She had never seen such a variety of spring flowers, such color. She took a deep breath and it was like inhaling the fragrance of many perfumes. She found her low spirits being lifted by the beauty of it all. "What a marvelous gardener you must have!" she exclaimed.

Edward smiled at the tribute. "I am the gardener," he said. "The gardens are my favorite part of the work here at Caradoc Court."

"Surely you have some help," she said. "It is not possible that you could take care of all the gardens alone."

He steered her along a grassy path to another part of the gardens, and it was obvious that she had pleased him with her reaction to his work. "Oh, yes, I have a little help with the weeding, but I take care of the rest of it myself."

She looked around at this different section and, again, was amazed at the number of flowers, the variety. There was every imaginable blossom excepting . . .

"There are no roses!" she cried suddenly. "There is everything but roses."

He smiled again and said, "Come with me," and they went to yet another garden which was hidden behind tall hedges. This garden contained nothing but roses of every possible size and color. There were red rose bushes, climbing yellow roses, pink sweetheart roses . . .

"Oh!" she breathed, unable to speak. Sudden tears had come into her eyes. The garden reminded her so much of her father's rose garden at Egmont House and of the loving care with which he had tended his roses. She looked at Edward, trying to imagine him, like her father, spending long hours lavishing time and love on his favorite flowers, and she found, strangely, that she could. A little while ago, it would have been impossible for her even to think of Edward and her father at the same time, but now she could make comparisons between the two. But, she chided herself, it was the contrasts between the two which she must keep in mind.

She saw then that Edward was looking at her, a bemused expression on his face. "My roses make you unhappy?"

"No," she said, "they make me homesick for the rose gardens of Egmont House."

"I am sorry," he said. "That is, I am sorry you miss your home so much. Perhaps as time goes on . . ."

"I shall miss it even more," she said instantly. "There will never be a day in my life that I shall not wish to be at Egmont House rather than here, your lovely roses notwithstanding."

Edward did not reply. He took her by the arm again and led her out of the rose garden to another garden behind the west wing, but before she could make comment, a servant approached, a harried look upon his face. "Oh, ma'am," he said, appearing considerably relieved at having found her. "Sir Rolf wishes to see you. He has had everyone looking for you. Will you come to his room now?"

Jocelyn looked at Edward, hoping he would answer and say she was busy at the moment and could not come, but all Edward did was to break into a big laugh and say, "He probably thought you had run away again."

Jocelyn lowered her head. "I shall be in directly," she said. It seemed such a pity to ruin what was turning out to be a beautiful morning.

The servant left them and Jocelyn said to Edward, "I suppose I must go."

"Yes, I suppose you must," he said agreeably, angering her.

He could not possibly know, she reasoned, how much she dreaded seeing his brother, how much she detested the sight of her husband, therefore why should he not seem agreeable about it? Yet, she reasoned, he did know that she had run away rather than live as Sir Rolf's wife. Was it possible that he thought it all an act on her part, that in spite of what she had told him, she had really wanted the marriage?

Saying nothing further to him, she hurried into the house, thinking, perhaps I should have thanked him for showing me the gardens. He did, at least, interrupt his work to do that, regardless of what he thinks of me.

Why, she wondered, had he made those overtures of friendship to her? Was it only because—as he had stated —"We are now related, and I would much prefer to get on with my sister-in-law than not." She probably had been reading too much into the words at the time. Because she wanted so much to have a friend at Caradoc Court, she had taken his words at their face value . . . or almost. Later, when she had more time, she would have to consider their implications.

Anyway, she had learned a valuable lesson; she would know better in the future. She would weigh every word spoken to her in this hateful place, no matter who did the speaking.

She paused outside Sir Rolf's door, took a deep breath, and tried not to think of the repulsive man on the other side of the door. She knocked softly and her husband answered in a booming voice, "Come!"

She opened the door. "I understand you wanted to see me."

Sir Rolf was sitting in the middle of the bed, the usual half dozen pillows behind him. "You understand!" he said sarcastically. "Madam, it is my opinion that you have very little understanding of anything under the sun, and that includes the holy institution of matrimony."

"My understanding of marriage may have become, understandably, a bit distorted," she said heatedly, "but I think I have a true understanding of my husband."

He looked at her angrily for a moment, and then, surprisingly, the corners of his slack mouth turned upward and he laughed. "You have spirit, I see," he said, his smile fading as quickly as it had appeared, "but that is not always a good thing in a woman. The fact is, you have shown entirely too much of the wrong kind of spirit ever since the marriage ceremony. Like a nervous, fidgety mare, you need to have a little of that spirit broken." He moved about the bed.

"Damme, am I *never* going to be able to get out of this bed again?" He gave her an accusing look. "Well, come in and close the door. Are you just going to stand there like a servant waiting for orders?"

"You have not been in that bed very long," she said, fury rising within her at first being compared with a horse and then called, by implication, subservient. "I think perhaps you are exaggerating your illness."

His face turned a hue of reddish purple. "I shall show you . . ." He struggled to sit upright without the pillows as a prop, winced with pain, and then fell back, breathing in short, painful gasps.

"May I be so bold as to inquire why you wanted to see me?" she asked sweetly—too sweetly.

"God's nightshirt, woman! Does a man have to have a specific reason for wanting to see his wife? The day is half gone and not so much as a good morning from you."

He looked at her as though he expected an answer, but when she did not reply, he went on, "Beginning on the morrow, your greeting to me is to be the first of the day. You are to come to this room as soon as you awaken. That is as it should be . . . until I am able to get about again. After that, there will be no need for you to come here because I shall have moved into the rooms you now occupy. We shall be living together in connubial bliss. Now then, do you understand *that*, my pretty?"

She felt her cheeks grow hot and wondered briefly if it was from anger or from the thought of sharing her apartment—her bed—with that great lump of a man. She turned her eyes away from him, unable to continue looking at him, and stared unseeingly at one of the grinning gargoyles. She had just learned another of her husband's traits: He could not bear to be bested by anyone, neither in conversation nor in anything else.

She turned, fumblingly opened the door, and left the room. But even through the massive oak door, she could hear his triumphant laughter as she ran down the hall to the safety of her own room—soon not to be so safe. His laughter sounded triumphant, she supposed, because he had finally succeeded in riling her beyond endurance.

Eight

After rising early Edward went to the dining room expectantly, thinking perhaps Jocelyn might be there, but she was not. There was only Hugo, the butler, waiting to serve his breakfast. Edward had not seen Jocelyn since she left him in the garden yesterday to go to Rolf. He assumed she had eaten the evening meal in her rooms.

"Has Mrs. Caradoc been in this morning?" he asked.

"Her abigail took breakfast to her, sir," Hugo answered.

Edward felt a moment of sharp disappointment, and he realized that without knowing it, he had been looking forward to seeing her. It would have been nice to have had her company at the beginning of the day. Also, he had wanted to be sure that she had not fared too badly when Rolf had sent for her.

As he ate, his thoughts went deeper and deeper into the subject of Jocelyn. Her behavior yesterday had left him baffled. Just when he had thought she was beginning to warm to his friendly overtures, she had once again returned to her manner of icy reserve which he knew was in some way supposed to be a rebuke to him. But for what? He had apologized to her, and he thought the apology had been accepted. And then she had turned from him and had gone into the house without a word, leaving him feeling that a chill winter wind had blown across his face. It was clear to him that her sudden change had not been entirely because of Rolf's summons, but because of something he himself had done or said.

The more he thought about it, the more he wanted the matter straightened out. The situation at Caradoc Court might not be happy for anyone right now, but it could be less miserable if he and Jocelyn could be friends —a great deal less miserable for both of them. As for those nagging doubts about her which remained in the back of his mind—he would try to see that they remained there.

As soon as he finished his breakfast, he went to the west wing to the door of her apartment, knocked, and then wondered at his appalling lack of consideration. It was possible that the tirade of abuse from Rolf yesterday had made her turn not only against Rolf but also against Rolf's brother.

He was about to turn and hurry away when the door was opened—not by the abigail, as he expected, but by Jocelyn herself. She looked at him questioningly.

"I was . . . I was just . . ." he began, and then realized that he had not the faintest notion what he was going to say to her or what he had had in mind when he came to her door. "I was wondering if you would like to go for a ride," he said, finally. "You saw the gardens yesterday, and I thought you might like to see something of the land belonging to the estate today."

She did not answer for a minute, and he could tell she was trying to decide not only whether to go with him, but possibly whether even to speak to him.

"Would that not be an unnecessary interruption to your work?" she asked, her tone stiff and formal.

"Looking over the land occasionally is part of my

work," he said, "and it would be most pleasant to have company."

Again she hesitated, and for such a long time that he said, "See here, Jocelyn, I meant it sincerely when I said yesterday that I should like us to be friends. And I thought you had agreed. If I have done or said something to offend you . . ."

"Let's speak no more about it," she said quickly. "I shall get my cloak and meet you in the courtyard. A ride would be quite the thing and I thank you for asking me."

Sir Rolf awoke later than usual and, for some reason, in much better spirits than he had been at any time since finding on his wedding day that his bride had disappeared. The pain in his back and leg seemed considerably diminished, and it was possible he would not have to remain in bed for the full month the doctor had deemed necessary for complete recovery.

He pushed himself up from his pillows, waited for a moment to be sure the pain was not going to engulf him, then he pulled the bell-cord for his valet. John appeared almost immediately with his breakfast tray and a soft-spoken, "Good morning, sir. I hope you are better today."

"We shall see," Sir Rolf muttered. He did not believe in getting too friendly or familiar with his servants. They were, at all times, to be fully aware of who was master. "I am going to get out of bed and have my breakfast in that chair by the window. Help me, will you?"

"Oh, sir! Are you sure you should? The doctor said . . ."

"To blazes with the doctor! I know better how I am feeling than he does. Here, give me a hand."

John put his arm just under Sir Rolf's arms and, bearing most of the weight, helped him from bed to chair. He hesitated once when Sir Rolf groaned, but Sir Rolf snapped, "Well, are you going to leave me suspended here? Keep moving, man!"

The pain returned to his leg as soon as he put his foot on the floor and to his back when he tried to walk, but he was determined to make it to the chair and, with John's help, he did. He emitted a long sigh, partly from pain, partly from satisfaction at being out of bed, as John placed the tray across the arms of the chair.

He was better, much better. He had known instinctively from the moment he woke up that he would be, and that was the cause of his improved spirits. Perhaps in a week, two weeks at most, he could play the part of bridegroom in actuality instead of merely in his mind. Then his bride truly would know who was lord and master of the manor and her husband as well.

His thoughts changed suddenly as he remembered that she had not come to his room this morning as he had bade her yesterday. He felt his anger rising, but then he thought that since he had overslept, she might have come earlier without his knowing it. He turned to John. "Go to my wife's apartment and tell her she may come back here now."

John left, then returned quickly. "Mrs. Caradoc has just gone out, sir. Her abigail said she has gone for a ride."

Sir Rolf leaned forward and peered out the window down into the courtyard. Yes, there was Jocelyn being helped into the carriage by Edward!

Damme! he thought, I shall not put up with this conduct either from her or from him. "Go outside and fetch her here immediately!" he thundered at John, and his valet took off at a run. But from the window Sir Rolf could see that it was too late. Edward jumped into the carriage and the two of them were rolling out of the courtyard and down the avenue to the highway before John arrived.

Sir Rolf was seething with wrath. The two of them, going off together while he, crippled by an accident caused by the aloof, hostile Jocelyn, was forced to sit here in his pain and watch! Well, he would put an abrupt halt to whatever they were planning against him—and it was obvious that if they were together, they had anything but his best interests at heart. What difference did it make to either of them, his wife *or* his brother, if he were here suffering while they drove about the countryside enjoying themselves? He could and would put a stop to any unnecessary association between Edward and Jocelyn, and he would do so immediately.

He said to John: "The instant my wife returns, you are to fetch her here to me. The very *instant!*"

As the carriage left the courtyard, Jocelyn felt her spirits lift, and as they drove down the wide, tree-lined avenue, she began to feel almost exuberant. Possessed of a naturally sunny disposition, her mood of the past few weeks had been as foreign to her as would have been a sudden change in her appearance.

At first, she had not wanted to come with Edward; she thought it would be awkward for her to be in the presence of one who thought so poorly of her. He would have her at a decided disadvantage. However, after considering it for a minute or two, she decided that as long as he had made the gesture, she could do no less than to accept. Ostensibly, they had declared an end to hostilities yesterday in the garden, and whatever he thought of her, he was managing a good outward show of friendliness. She could at least do the same. Her life had enough unpleasantness in it right now without adding even one whit of animosity if she could help it.

Now she was glad that she had come. Edward was smiling and looking more relaxed than she had ever seen him as he pointed out special trees and flowers along the way. Was it possible that he, too, felt the oppressive atmosphere of Caradoc Court and was as glad to get away —even temporarily—as she?

"You see that tree?" he was saying. "It is a type of cedar, and we have no idea how old it is—several hundred years at least, and . . . My dear Jocelyn, you are actually smiling. Do you know I have never seen you with a real smile on your face before?"

"And you are also," she said. "You are like a different person now that we are away from Caradoc Court. Do you not like your own home?"

He sat up a little, then turned toward her. "To be truthful, I have not felt that that house was my home since Rolf changed it so much a number of years ago. It does not look like the same house, inside or out. It does not even *feel* like the same house." He leaned back again. "Anyway, it is not the same place in which I grew up. *That* house was mine—as much mine as Rolf's. But the changes he made took away all of the things I liked best about the house, so now it is his home and I feel, most of the time, that I am merely a visitor—and sometimes not a very welcome one."

"Did not . . ." she hesitated, unable at first to get the hated words out, but finally she managed, "Did not my husband consult you before the changes were made? My understanding is that the house is yours also."

"Rolf seldom consults anyone when there is something he wants," Edward said bitterly. "Whether it be a house, a horse . . . or a wife."

She looked down at her hands, clenched tightly in her lap. "I do not think it would be necessary for him to consult you about either a horse or a wife," she said sharply. "But about the house, yes."

"I am sorry," he said. "I—I did not mean to offend you. I only meant to point out that my brother never consults anyone about anything, and that is something you will learn about him soon enough."

She turned her head, appearing to be studying the scenery carefully in order not to have to answer him. Why was it that he—either intentionally or unintentionally, she was not sure which—always managed to arouse her ire? She had never thought she was overly sensitive and had almost never taken umbrage at what others said to her. Why then did almost everything Edward Caradoc say to her set her nerves on edge? After all, he was only the younger brother of the detestable Sir Rolf. Did she really care so much for his good opinion?

"I seem always to be apologizing to you for something I have said." He continued talking before the silence took on a degree of animosity. "Could I not simply make one big apology now for anything I said in the past which offended you and for anything I may say in the future which you might possibly take as an affront, and then let us forget this whole business of apologizing and go on about the business of being friends?"

She turned toward him again, took one look at the earnest expression on his face, and laughed. The idea of apologizing in advance for insults not yet even imagined struck her as very amusing. She told him so, and he, seeing that she was no longer angry, laughed heartily with her, and then they resumed their conversation. He told her how the house had been before his brother "decided to tamper with everything," and how he had always felt at home there because it was the only home he had ever known. "But now," he ended up, gesturing back in the direction of Caradoc Court, "I do not feel at home and never shall in that . . . that monstrosity."

"Nor I," she said. "I loathe the place and have from the first moment I saw it. I cannot even think of any circumstances under which I might like it. But, please, let us change the subject. It depresses me even to speak of it, and the countryside is so lovely and it is so pleasant to be riding in the opposite direction from Caradoc Court that I cannot bear to be depressed right now. That will come soon enough when we return."

"For both of us," he said. "I am beginning to feel that we are conspirators."

She laughed. "When I was a child, I sometimes felt that Gerard and I were conspirators when we were trying to hide some incident from our parents. Was it ever like that with you and . . . and my husband?"

"Hardly," Edward said. "Rolf is eighteen years older than I. He was an adult by the time I was old enough to understand anything."

"More like a second father, perhaps?"

"No." He shook his head. "To be truthful, Rolf and I saw no more of each other then than we do now . . . less, probably. He was always gallivanting around the countryside or making trips to London. Even when he was at home, our paths seldom crossed. No one could ever call us close as brothers."

"Oh, look!" Jocelyn pointed suddenly to a field where several lambs tottered on spindly, unsteady legs. "Look at the dear little things!"

Edward nodded. "There are more on the other side of the flock. See there! Lambing time was later than usual this spring."

They rode in silence for a few minutes, a congenial silence this time, while Jocelyn looked all about, first on one side of the road and then the other, enjoying the sights and smells of the country. And yet, her enjoyment was hampered by the thought, never far from the surface of her mind, that soon they would be returning to the dark, depressing house and that no doubt Sir Rolf would send for her to give her another tonguelashing for not going to his room to bid him good-morning. She had deliberately disobeyed him.

"You must have been happy here as a boy," she said finally. "All this land to ride about, all the animals, the gardens . . ."

"Happy enough, I suppose," he said. "My mother died the day I was born, the sixteenth of September, 1790, and my father was usually busy about the estate. As I said, I seldom saw Rolf, but I would say I had a very contented childhood. Occasionally my father would take me with him when he expected to be out all day and the cook would pack a box meal for us . . ." He broke off and snapped his fingers. "Oh, drat! Why did I not think of that today? We could have eaten in the meadow yonder."

She shook her head, knowing instinctively that her husband would have gone into a rage worse than any she had witnessed so far. "It is nearly time to eat now," she said. "Should we not be getting back?"

"I suppose so," he agreed reluctantly. "Do you take your meals with Rolf? I have not seen you in the dining room."

"No, I have a tray brought to my room," she said.

"Then perhaps you would join me at meal time. It can be a lonely feeling, always eating alone."

"Did you and . . . and my husband not eat together before his accident?"

"Almost never," he said. "I usually rise earlier than he in the morning; at noon I am always busy with the books or else out overseeing some of the work, and at night Rolf is almost never at home. I am sure that will change, though, now that he has a wife to be more company for him than I have been."

She thought, I can imagine that he was away at night as easily as I can imagine what he was doing, but she said nothing. Sir Rolf and Edward were, after all, brothers, and it certainly behooved her not to fall into the habit of talking about one brother to the other. For all she knew, Edward could be every bit the reprobate his brother was, even though, at this point, he did not seem to be.

He clucked to the horses as he slapped the reins lightly over their backs. For a moment Jocelyn had the feeling that not even the horses wanted to go back.

She was no sooner in the house than John, her husband's valet, stopped her on the way to her apartment and told her that Sir Rolf wished to see her immediately.

She went straight to his door and knocked, and when he bellowed "Come!" she knew that his foul mood was not concerned entirely with her absence this morning. However, she entered his room with a smile on her face and said "Good-morning," cheerfully.

"It is near enough to afternoon that I think you could change your greeting," Sir Rolf said, scowling.

"I am delighted to see you sitting in a chair instead of the bed," she said, seeming to ignore the increasing signs of storm.

"Sit down," he said, pointing to a chair opposite his. "You never seem to want to sit down when you are in this room."

She sat down, still smiling. "You have looked to be in such pain, and I did not wish to tire you further by a long visit." She was determined not only to be civil to him, but also pleasant.

"If you have any memory at all, I am sure you will

recall our conversation yesterday," he said, obviously thrown off by her cordiality. "You agreed to come here to see me the first thing every morning."

"Oh, no," she said quickly. "You *told* me to come here, but I did not agree."

The signs of rage returned, and it was clear to her that he was scarcely able to control his voice when he said, "Then, madam, I shall have your agreement now. You are to have your breakfast here, in this room with me, every morning and you will stay an hour or more. And in the afternoons you will return for another hour, and then you will have the evening meal here. I will not have you traipsing or riding about with my brother while I am shut in here because of you. Is that understood?"

"Perfectly," she said, having difficulty now in keeping her own voice steady.

"And do not think you can get away with not coming," he continued. "If you are not here when you are supposed to be, I shall send every servant in the house to look for you, and, believe me, I shall see to it that you are grossly humiliated."

She did not answer but thought: Marriage to you was enough humiliation to last me a lifetime.

Apparently, something about the way she was looking made him relent somewhat, and when he spoke again both his tone of voice and his words were kinder. "Really, my dear, if you would not continually oppose me, you would find that I am not the ogre you think I am. Why, I was thinking just this morning how nice it would be for us to take a drive together, and I had a splendid idea. As soon as I am able to leave this room—and that may be sooner than we thought—I am going to buy a phaeton for you, just for your use, and one of the stable men can be your driver. Then, we can go for long rides together, or you can go alone when it is not convenient for me. Now, do you see how I am constantly trying to think of things for your pleasure?"

She could not but compare him with Edward as a companion on a drive through the countryside, and the thought of sitting beside him and listening to him talk almost made her cringe visibly.

"Why do you not answer?" he barked. "Are you a complete ingrate?"

She gave a long, listless sigh. "I am suddenly very tired," she said. "I came straight here from my drive this morning and I would like to go to my rooms and freshen up a bit."

"Go then," he said, "but remember, you are to be back this afternoon, and if you do not return . . ."

She left before he could finish the threat. She should resign herself to her new life, she thought, and stop trying to avoid seeing her husband. There was no way she could change their relationship any more than she could change the pattern of her new life. Resignation was the only way left to her.

She looked up just before opening the door to her apartment, and there was Edward, standing dead still in the center of the hallway, staring at her.

"Jocelyn, you are so pale," he said. "What did Rolf say to you?"

She opened her mouth and started to tell him, but found that she could not speak without bursting into tears, so she hurried into her room and closed the door without answering.

After John told Jocelyn that Rolf wanted to see her immediately, Edward purposely had waited in the hall for Jocelyn to emerge from his brother's room, knowing whatever Rolf had to say to her could not, by any stretch of the imagination, be construed as good news. He was not prepared, however, for the pale, distraught-looking Jocelyn who came out. And when she disappeared into her apartment without answering his question, his first impulse was to follow her and comfort her for . . . he knew not what.

His second impulse was to rush into Rolf's room and demand to know what he had done or said to the poor girl. This was the impulse which he followed.

Rolf stared at him, a rather amused look in his eyes. "So you want to know what goes on between my wife and me, do you? I do not suppose for a moment that you have stopped to consider that this is no concern of yours."

This stopped Edward cold, as he realized the truth of his brother's words. He tried to calm himself somewhat, knowing that if his anger really became aroused, he could be as formidable as Rolf. "I was merely alarmed," he said slowly, "when I saw her rush from this room in a state of some agitation. I naturally could not help but wonder what you might have said to her."

"I will tell you what I said to her if it will ease your mind," Rolf said. "I told her that as soon as I am able to leave this room, I would buy her a phaeton, and that she could have one of the men at the stables to drive her about. Now, does that sound like anything that would distress the lovely Jocelyn?"

Not only the sarcasm in Rolf's voice, but also the way he said "the lovely Jocelyn" riled Edward. He knew that unless he left immediately, he would lose his temper completely. Yet he did not go.

"I think you must have said something else," he said. "I am *certain* you said something else."

"As I said before, it is no concern of yours." Rolf deliberately turned his back on his brother and looked out the window. Edward was too furious to trust himself to say anything else. He merely looked at the back of Rolf's head, wishing he could strike his brother, knock him completely out of the chair.

In a moment Rolf turned again. "I am going to tell you something, Edward, and I want you to listen well. I saw you driving out with my wife this morning, and I know to the minute how long you were out with her. I would remind you that she is *my* wife, but I am sure you have not sufficient scruples to let that fact bother you. In the future . . . in fact, beginning this very instant . . . you are to stay as far away as possible from Jocelyn. There will be no more drives about the countryside, no more walks in the gardens. I do not want you even to *speak* to her except in my presence. I am well aware that you have been attracted to her from the beginning, and I warn you now that if you do not either get over or conceal this attraction, I shall call you out as soon as I am able to leave this room . . . even though you are my brother."

Edward advanced toward the chair, stopping himself just before raising his arm to Rolf. His fury was at such a point now that he could not have uttered a word had he wanted to.

Rolf, seeing his torment, laughed. "You may go now, Edward," he said. "Jocelyn will be returning shortly, and I would like to get a little rest before then."

Edward stalked to the door, then turned. "You are a blithering idiot," he raged. "You have not the slightest notion what you are talking about. You are completely mad. Completely. And yet you still manage to become more insane every day. I do not quite see how that is possible, yet . . ." Choking with anger, he could say no more. He went out, slamming the door after him so hard that the noise reverberated all through the west wing of the house.

By the time he had walked to his own room in the east wing, he had calmed down somewhat, and his mind was wholly occupied with something else, something Rolf had said. *You have been attracted to her from the beginning.*

He thought about Jocelyn now . . . as she had been the day he had called at Egmont House to deliver the ring, her almost numbed look at the wedding, her seeming distraction during the wedding breakfast. And then he thought of her as they had walked through the rose garden, as she had been this morning when they had gone out in the carriage, leaving Caradoc Court behind them.

And he thought about the possibility that she might actually have tried to do Rolf bodily harm after making a mercenary marriage. Somehow, this last thought seemed unreal, not worth considering. Yet he knew that some day, possibly some day soon, he was going to have to consider it very seriously.

But for now . . . Good Lord! he thought, Rolf is right. Without knowing it, I have been attracted to her since the first day I saw her.

His mind had hardly grasped this before another thought came and all but overwhelmed him. It was more than mere attraction. His feeling for Jocelyn deepened every time he saw her, in spite of those reservations about her which he tried to keep in the back of his mind.

Oh God! he thought, this cannot be possible; this cannot be true.

But even as he thought it, he knew it was both possible and true. He had fallen in love with his brother's wife.

Nine

Spring turned into summer, and the days lengthened. To Jocelyn each day was like the one before, and she could have sworn that she was aware of the few more minutes of daylight, for the longer the day, the longer her torment lasted. She obeyed Sir Rolf's orders to the letter, for she was aware of what disobedience would mean to her—and to Gerard. Each morning she went to Sir Rolf's room for breakfast, and then later in the morning, returned and sat with him for exactly one hour; and then in the late afternoon she returned for another hour, remaining to eat with him again. She could not have told what she was eating, for her mind was never on the food, only on how miserable she was. She seldom spoke, replying to his rare question to her only in monosyllables, but he talked incessantly. Usually, his monologues consisted of stories of his adventures in London and abroad, and about how ladies everywhere set their caps for him, egged on by their eager mothers. Jocelyn listened to his distasteful boasting wtihout a change of expression, though she knew he was lying most of the time. She had heard, only too many times, how unacceptable Sir Rolf had been, not only to the young ladies, but also to their families. And never, during those hearings, did it occur to her that she would be the unlucky one who would end up as mistress of Caradoc Court.

With each passing day, Jocelyn became more and more puzzled by Edward's strange behavior. He had seemed sincere in wanting to be friends with his sister-in-law and yet, ever since the day they had gone for a ride in the carriage together, he had obviously been avoiding her. He had suggested that they have meals together in the small dining room, yet when she went there at midday—the only meal she did not have to eat in Sir Rolf's room—he was never there. If she happened to meet him in the halls or, as happened once or twice, in the gardens, he gave her a formal bow, a cheerful "good-morning" or "good-afternoon," and walked quickly away from her as though afraid she might be the carrier of a dread disease.

She was not only perplexed but also hurt, because she had so wanted to have a friend here, someone besides Irva to whom she could talk freely, and for a very short while, she thought she had found that friend in Edward. She could not imagine what had caused the sudden— indeed, overnight—change in him for he had seemed to be as lonely, as out of place in that terrible house as she. Several times—twice in the house and once in the garden—she had come upon him and had spoken enthusiastically, but when, on each occasion, his answer had seemed more rebuff than reply, she vowed she would avoid him whenever possible and that if they should meet by accident again, she would be as cold and remote as he.

Every day was so much like every other day that Jocelyn soon lost all track of time. Only once during her first weeks in her new home was there an incident to make the day different, and that was not quite three weeks after her marriage.

During the morning hour with Sir Rolf, he looked at

her piercingly and stopped talking. "I do not think you are listening to a word I am saying."

"Oh yes," she said hastily. "I hear every word you say." It was true, she heard his voice, even though she was not concentrating on what he was saying.

"Why are you distracted?" he persisted. "What were you thinking about while I was talking to you?"

"I was listening," she said, seeing that he was on the verge of anger. "What would I be thinking about except what you are talking about?" And she thought, what indeed? About Edward's odd change toward her, about Egmont House, about her homesickness . . .

His expression changed to a more benign one and he leaned forward in his chair and patted her hand. "I had not thought of it before," he said, "but I suppose my injuries are inconvenient for you also. At least, you are somewhat confined as well as I. So, my dear, I have a surprise for you." With that, he pulled himself up by the arms of his chair, turned slowly and walked to the window, then back to the chair. She watched him in amazement, for although he had been out of bed, seated in the chair, every time she came to his room, she had not seen him so much as take a step without a servant on either side supporting him.

"Has the pain gone entirely from your back and leg?" she asked.

"No, but it is less," he said. "I can get around by myself. For that matter, I see no reason why we should not go for a ride together this afternoon, do you?"

She could not answer. She stared at him, a sudden thought rendering her speechless. She was glad his pain was less, glad he could now get around without aid, but the fact that he was better also meant that before too much longer, she would be his wife in more than name. He would soon be moving into "her" apartment, sharing the big, canopied bed with her. The thought made her blood run cold.

"I said, how would you like to go for a ride with me this afternoon?" he repeated. "Perhaps we can go as far as the village where I shall put in an order for a phaeton for you." He seemed in such unusually good spirits that she tried to speak enthusiastically; it was seldom enough, Lord knew, that he was even civil. "I think that would be very nice," she said. "Quite the thing."

He beamed at her as though he had just granted her the earth, and she had thanked him for it. "Now," he said, "I have another surprise for you. I shall accompany you to the dining room and take my meal there with you." With that, he grasped her arm and escorted her out of the room.

Although they walked very slowly, Sir Rolf did not limp much, but he did wince with pain once or twice before they reached the dining room. As they entered, Edward was just getting up from the table. "Well, Rolf," he said. "This is quite a surprise. Ought you to be walking so far?"

"I am sure you would rather I did not walk at all," Sir Rolf replied, obviously put out at seeing Edward there. "But I assure you I am quite in practice. I have been walking about my room for several days now." With that, he took his hand from Jocelyn's arm and advanced alone, at a faster pace, as though to prove himself as fit as his brother. However, just before reaching the table, his left leg gave way and he toppled to the floor, an expression of pain and complete surprise on his face.

"Oh!" Jocelyn cried, running to him.

Edward reached down, as though to help his brother up, then turned instead and told Hugo to go immediately for the doctor. "You had better remain there," he said, "at least until the doctor arrives."

"Nonsense!" Sir Rolf said. "Help me up this instant. My leg is simply weak from not being used much."

With Jocelyn on one side and Edward on the other, they managed to get him to his feet, but he was obviously in much pain, grimacing as they helped him to a chair. "I am not hungry," he said. "I think I shall go back to my room."

He was taken back by two servants—literally taken—when it became apparent that he could bear no weight on his left leg.

"Sit down and eat," Edward told Jocelyn. "I have finished and I will wait with Rolf for the doctor. There is nothing you can do."

She did as she was told, but the meal was tasteless to her, and five minutes after leaving the table she could not have told what she ate. She reached her husband's room just as John was showing the doctor in, so she waited in the hall.

In a few minutes Edward came out. "It is not too serious," he said. "He was trying to be too active too soon. The doctor says he should have given his leg and back more time to heal. Now, he will have to stay in bed at least another month."

Jocelyn was aware that she was smiling, but she was not sure whether the reason for the smile was because her husband was not seriously hurt . . . . or because he would remain confined to his room for another month. Or, maybe, because Edward had had more to say to her than at any time since the afternoon they had gone out in the carriage. Perhaps, once again, she might look forward to having a friend in the house.

She found out the next day, however, that the hope had been in vain. After breakfast, as she was leaving Sir Rolf's room, she met Edward just going in. "Good-morning," she said, and the thought occurred to her that Edward might think of asking her to go out for a ride, or perhaps a walk in the gardens to break the monotony for her.

It was apparent that Edward had no such intention, though, when he answered her greeting with a nod and said only, "I trust Rolf is feeling better today." Without waiting for her answer, he went into the room, closing the door behind him.

Tears sprang to her eyes, and she went to her apartment and asked Irva to walk with her in the gardens.

When it became obvious to Jocelyn that Edward was studiously avoiding her—though it was not obvious to her why—she became even more depressed and homesick. She could not go near Edward's rose garden without crying for the rose garden at Egmont House. Every time she saw the carriage leave the courtyard, whether it contained Edward or a servant going to the village on an errand, she wished that she were in it—on her way home. Her homesickness became so acute that she could get her mind on nothing else during the day, and at night she lay awake trying to think of some way she could leave Caradoc Court forever.

She realized that these thoughts were a useless waste of time, for there was no way she could escape without putting Gerard's life in danger. Gerard had told her and Sir Rolf had intimated that if she left, it was entirely possible that Gerard would pay with his life.

Once she thought of being so disagreeable that Sir Rolf would want her to go, would want to get rid of her, but then she knew that that was exactly what he would do, "get rid of her," but not in the way she wanted. If he had threatened Gerard's life if she tried to leave, how much worse it would be for her! She had been around Sir Rolf long enough now to know he was a man who, one way

or another, would get what he wanted and would see
that those who tried to stand in his way suffered.

Edward was no happier than Jocelyn with the state of
affairs at Caradoc Court, but he knew he could register no
emotion, let absolutely no one suspect his feelings toward
his sister-in-law. It was not because he was afraid of
Rolf, but because he knew that his brother would take
out any and every frustration, angry thought, or disappointment on Jocelyn, and he wanted to spare her as much
as possible.

It cut him like a knife to have to ignore or avoid her, but
he knew this was his only course of action. Until he
found out that she had her breakfast in Rolf's room every
morning, he had eaten early in order to avoid her in
the dining room. Now, he went only to his midday meal
early, knowing that was the only meal she ate in the
dining room. When he met her about the house or outside, it was all he could do to keep from taking her in his
arms and stroking her dark hair as though she were a
child, saying "There, there, it is going to be all right, dear
Jocelyn." He wanted to comfort her, console her, love
her . . .

But he could not tell her everything was going to be all
right for that would be a lie. Nothing would ever be all
right again—for either of them. She would remain here
in this place she hated for the rest of her life, married
to his brother, and he would remain here for the rest of
his life, miserably loving her and being unable to do anything about it.

These were the thoughts that preyed on his mind day
in, day out. Rolf's accident in the dining room was only a
slight distraction. As far as Edward could tell after talking
with the doctor, the accident had done little damage
to anything except Rolf's already weak control of his

temper. True, his brother would have to keep to his room for another month, but that was only postponing the inevitable. Eventually he would leave the room and move into the apartment he had fixed up for himself and Jocelyn.

He went to Rolf's room the morning after the doctor's visit to see what frame of mind his brother was in, and he found out as soon as he opened the door. Before he even had a chance to say good-morning, Rolf greeted him with, "I suppose you are a happy man today, Edward."

"Why do you say that?"

"You know as well as I do. You think you will have Jocelyn to yourself for another month."

"Except for an occasional good-morning, your wife and I have not exchanged a word for a fortnight. Until your fall yesterday, that is."

"A likely story! You need not bother to lie to me, Edward, for I can read you like a book."

Completely disgusted and sorry that he had come, Edward said, "It is my understanding that you have read few books in your life." With that he walked out without even bothering to inquire as to how his brother was feeling.

That morning he worked off his fury in the rose garden, hoping that Jocelyn would wander by and that he might at least get a glimpse of her. And glimpse her he did across the hedges that separated the roses from the rest of the flowers as she walked with her abigail, but she did not so much as look toward the rose garden and, therefore, she could not know that he was standing there, looking at her longingly.

A few days after that, Edward decided that although he was acting in an honorable way toward his brother and his brother's wife, he was also acting in an asinine way. Rolf had not believed him when he had told him he rarely saw or spoke to Jocelyn, so he might as well have been enjoying her company all this time. As for Rolf's threat that he would call him out, Edward knew it would never happen. Rolf would do everything he could to add to Edward's discomfort, to make his life miserable, but he would never do anything that would put his own life in jeopardy. In some ways, Rolf was a devout coward.

So, thinking that he might as well be hanged for a sheep as a lamb, Edward went looking for Jocelyn one morning to invite her to go for a drive with him. Her abigail opened the door when he knocked.

"Miss Jocelyn left a little while ago," Irva said. "She has gone for a walk. I don't know where."

Disappointed, but still determined, Edward went to his office in the east wing and sat by the window where he could see Jocelyn when she returned. He would ask her then, and Rolf be damned!

Jocelyn wandered aimlessly, unaware and not caring where she went. After she had ambled through the gardens she had decided that she would like to walk farther. The thought of going back inside the house was comparable to the thought of freely entering a dungeon. So she had entered the woods behind the house at almost the same place she had gone in after the wedding breakfast, but this time she knew where the path was, and she kept to it.

There was no thought in her mind now of wild animals, or of any other harm she might encounter. She supposed her tranquil state of mind was due to the fact that she now considered anything that happened to her in the house far worse than anything she might encounter outside.

Several times she stopped walking and breathed deeply. The scent of the evergreens was strong and pleasant and refreshing. One thing surprised her greatly, however:

the deeper she went into the woods, the quieter the world around her became. By the time she was well into the forest, she did not even hear a bird call. This was a bit unnerving. It was as though every living thing in the forest had become silent because of her presence, and the silence gave her an eerie feeling.

She did not know how long or how far she had walked when she saw a cottage at the end of the path. Startled, she stopped and looked. Then she realized that this was the home of the woman who had helped her and Sir Rolf the night he had fallen from his horse (she refused to think of it as her wedding night). What was her name? Maeve something. Then she remembered, Maeve Mc-Caulay, the seamstress for Caradoc Court.

She went on a few steps and saw the woman herself sitting on a bench in front of the cottage, her sewing in her lap, her fingers moving busily over the material. Just as Jocelyn was trying to decide whether to turn back or to go on and speak to the woman, Maeve McCaulay spotted her and stood up, craning her neck as though to see better.

Jocelyn emerged from the woods in front of the cottage. She was about to speak, but the woman spoke first. "Oh, it's you, is it?" was her greeting. "What do you want here?"

"Good day, Mrs. McCaulay," Jocelyn said cheerfully in spite of the rude greeting. "I was out for a walk and did not realize I had come so far."

"Running away from your husband again, I take it." The woman was looking at her as though trying to see straight through her.

"Oh, no!" Jocelyn replied in a shocked tone, as though such a thought would never—*had* never—occurred to her. "Just out to get a little air."

"And in a minute or two Sir Rolf will come charging up to take you back."

"Sir Rolf has not yet recuperated from his fall on that night when you so graciously helped us," Jocelyn said.

The woman laughed. "That is no surprise. 'Tis a wonder he wasn't kilt. And no fault of yours that he wasn't."

From the way the woman spoke, it was impossible for Jocelyn to tell whether she was being chastised or congratulated. She changed the subject. "May I sit down and rest a bit before I start back?"

"Sit if you like." Mrs. McCaulay pushed a strand of gray hair away from her face as she looked down again at her sewing. Jocelyn saw that the material was heavy, certainly not material for a dress. "What are you making?" she asked.

"Draperies for Mr. Edward's new room," she answered.

"New room?" Jocelyn could not keep the surprise out of her voice. It occurred to her now, for the first time, that the bedroom she had seen in the east wing, the one which definitely did not belong to one of the servants, was Edward's.

"You never knew, I take it, that Mr. Edward moved into the east wing just before you and Sir Rolf . . . just before you were married."

"No," Jocelyn said stonily. "I had no idea."

"I imagine there's a good bit that goes on that you have no idea about," Mrs. McCaulay said.

"I am sure there is," Jocelyn said. "I cannot, after all, be everywhere at once and know everything that goes on."

The woman began laughing and did not stop until forced to by a cough. "That's the God's truth," she said, agreeably, for once. "If you could, you never would have come to Caradoc Court at all."

"I had no choice in the matter," Jocelyn said before she thought, then added hastily, "That is, I had never seen Caradoc Court until the day I came here to be married." She most assuredly was not going to let this seamstress know that her brother had sold her into bondage to Sir Rolf as surely as if she had been a slave.

"And my guess is that you had never seen Sir Rolf either," the woman nodded, a smug expression on her face.

"Oh, yes," Jocelyn said quickly, too quickly. "I had seen him before." She stood up, having no desire to discuss her marriage with this woman who was not only a stranger to her, but hardly more than a servant.

Maeve McCaulay looked at her and smiled a knowing sort of smile. "Sit down, dearie. There's nothing you can tell me about Sir Rolf that I don't know already. The truth is, I could probably tell you a few things."

Jocelyn did not sit down again, but neither did she leave.

"Still laid up from his fall, is he?" Maeve continued conversationally. "I've no doubt that pleases you as much as it displeases him. Well, I suppose we can just mark it all up to the many strange goings-on in that house."

"What do you mean by that?" Jocelyn asked. "You are implying that something is amiss . . ."

"I am implying nothing," the woman said impatiently. "I am telling you plainly that things are not as they should be in that house. Never have been, as far as I can remember, and I've been here for twenty-four years."

A cold chill ran through Jocelyn as she detected a sinister note in the seamstress's words. "What are you talking about?" she whispered. "How could you possibly know what goes on at Caradoc Court . . . unless some of the servants tell you?" she added as an afterthought.

Maeve had a raucous laugh. "How indeed? Dearie, I hope it wasn't for love that you married Sir Rolf, because it is not likely he will ever love anyone more than himself. Of course, one can readily see why he married you, a pretty thing who can give him the heir he has always wanted. No, come back. I have something to say, something that will interest you, maybe help you to understand what goes on at Caradoc Court better."

Jocelyn, who had started to move away when Maeve's observations became personal, stopped. "What could you possibly tell me about the place that I do not know already?"

"Ha! Sit down. You'll see."

Jocelyn sat down beside the woman on the bench again.

"I seem to feel a bit sorry for you, my girl, though I am not sure why," Maeve said patronizingly. "Maybe because you are young, a bit scared, and very unhappy . . ."

"I am not . . ." Jocelyn began.

"Of course you're unhappy," Maeve interrupted cheerfully. "One has only to look at you. Anyway, so you won't find out for yourself and be in for a rude awakening, I am going to tell you something." She paused a moment, nodding her head as though trying to decide how to say what was on her mind. Then she continued, "Have you ever been in the chapel, the south wing of the house?"

"I was married to Sir Rolf in that chapel."

"Ah, yes, you would be, wouldn't you? Now let me tell you about the chapel. It was built when Sir Rolf decided to change the whole house, and it was built over the family graves. There is a little stairway to the left of the altar that leads down to the graves. If you will go down that stairway, you will be in for a surprise."

"What is so surprising about family graves?" Jocelyn asked.

"You will see what you will see," Maeve said. "And if you don't see it, come back to see me and I will tell you what to look for." She resumed sewing with exaggerated concentration.

Jocelyn, knowing that the woman would say nothing else, stood up. "I must be going back. Good-by, Mrs.

McCaulay." As she walked back to the path in the woods, the woman gave another raucous laugh and called, "Call me Maeve. Everybody does." And she was still laughing when Jocelyn passed out of earshot.

A strange woman, Jocelyn thought as she walked back in the direction she had come. A thoroughly unpleasant woman, and yet . . . No, she had not really been unpleasant. A little rude, perhaps. A bit presumptuous.

Why had she told Jocelyn about the graves beneath the chapel? Was there some skeleton she wanted the mistress of Caradoc Court to find? Jocelyn shuddered at her own choice of words. Of course, there was really nothing amiss. What earth-shaking bit of information could be found among some old graves of the deceased members of Caradoc Court? Whatever secrets those Caradocs knew had certainly been sealed by their deaths.

However, just to satisfy her curiosity, she would look under the chapel when she got back to the house.

But as she crossed the courtyard, she heard her name called and she turned. Edward, standing at a door in the east wing, threw up his hand.

"I have been waiting for you," he said, coming toward her. "I thought you might like to go for a short drive with me."

For a moment she was too surprised to answer. She had long since decided that there would be no more friendly overtures from Edward, and this unexpected invitation startled her.

"I say short drive because I know Rolf expects you in his room this afternoon," Edward continued. "We can return in good time for your visit with him."

"Thank you, but I think perhaps I had better not," she said. She knew only too well that if her husband found that she had been for a ride with Edward again, he would put even more restrictions on her free time.

"Oh, come," Edward said persuasively. "I shall have the carriage fetch us outside the courtyard, so Rolf will not know. I think it would do us both good just to get away for a little while."

"I have already been away for a while," she told him. "I am just returning from a long walk."

"Do you have to give account for every minute of the day?" Edward asked.

"No, but . . ." And then she thought: What more can Sir Rolf say that he has not already said? To ride about the countryside and get away from this depressing place, to have Edward's company for a little while, is worth risking an hour's tantrum this afternoon.

She smiled at him and said, "All right, I will go. I shall be delighted."

Ten

Jocelyn, feeling a little guilty, met Edward at the carriage house which was beside the stables. There was no way Sir Rolf could see them from his room. Edward smiled at her like a coconspirator as he handed her into the carriage. "No need for worry," he said. "We will be back before Rolf knows you have gone."

"I cannot help worrying a little," she said as they started down the avenue to the highway. "But even if he finds out, it will be worth whatever unpleasantness occurs just to get away for a little while."

Edward looked at her closely. He seemed, in fact, to be studying her, as though trying to read her mind and having difficulty in doing so. His forehead was lined with tiny furrows, and his dark brows were raised in an attitude of questioning, but he said nothing.

"What is it?" she asked. "Is something bothering you?"

"I think we will go in the opposite direction today," he said, ignoring her questions. "We will go toward the village, though not that far, of course."

She nodded, wondering why he had not given her an answer, what it was that he would not share with her. They rode in silence for a while, and she noticed that every now and then he turned his head and looked at

139

her, looking away when she returned his stare. Finally she said, "What *is* it, Edward? It is perfectly obvious that something is bothering you."

"Nothing," he said. "There is nothing bothering me."

"You said some time ago that you wanted us to be friends," she said. "How can we be friends if you do not trust me enough to tell me what is on your mind?"

He laughed as though she had said something extremely amusing, then he said, "I am not sure we would be friends if I told you what is on my mind. Seriously, nothing is bothering me; 'puzzling' would be a better word. I am very puzzled about something."

"What is it?"

He hesitated for a moment, looked away, then looked back at her. "I have been wondering more and more how you came to be married to Rolf. Until recently, before I got to know you better, I assumed it was for the money, but it stands to reason that it was not, or you would not have tried to run away right after the wedding."

His words came as no surprise to her. He had made it obvious in the beginning that he thought her mercenary, a fortune seeker. The surprise was in the fact that he did not know about the marriage contract, but then, when she stopped to think about that, she realized that Sir Rolf probably would not have told anyone about the contract, not even his brother, for fear of losing face.

"Your first assumption was correct," she said lightly. "It was for the money." She waited a moment, enjoying immensely the look of shock on his face, then she added, "But it was for my brother, not for me."

Then she told him the whole story, leaving out no detail, about Gerard's gambling debts, about the deal he had made with Sir Rolf knowing that Sir Rolf wanted a wife, about the marriage contract, and about the many ways she had tried to get out of it.

"I knew nothing about any of it until after the contract was signed," she said. "When I refused to go through with the wedding, Gerard told me that Sir Rolf would kill him—or have him killed—if he did not keep his part of the bargain. Then, after the wedding, I thought I had kept Gerard's part of the contract since it only stated that I must marry Sir Rolf, and so I tried to get away. That is why Sir Rolf went riding into the woods alone that night, to look for me. He did not even want the servants to know I had left him. I startled the horse, and Sir Rolf was thrown, and so he blames me for the accident."

Edward, who had been looking at her incredulously, nodded slowly now. "I am beginning to understand," he said, "except for one thing. You *did* keep your brother's part of the bargain by marrying Rolf, so how can he now hold you here?"

"My brother gets a monthly check from Sir Rolf and it will stop unless I remain at Caradoc Court," she said. "Also Gerard has said, and Sir Rolf has hinted, that if I leave, Sir Rolf will call Gerard out, or do harm to him in some other way." She could not bring herself to say the word "murder" even though she was sure that would be the final result if she ever tried to leave again. "You see, it is a hopeless situation. Hopeless for me, anyway."

"I had guessed you were married under duress, but I had not realized it was all so complicated," Edward said, "or that you had so little to do with any of it."

The change of expression on Edward's face was amazing to her. As she had talked, she had seen it change from worry, to interest, to . . . what was it now? Boyish delight? But how could he be delighted by the sordid story she had just told him? And then she thought she understood. He had really thought her marriage was, if not wanted, at least voluntary on her part in order to obtain Sir Rolf's fortune. Now, with her finally telling him the truth about the affair, he had exonerated her in his mind. She was sure that this was the case; he had actually been accusing her of God knew what immoralities in his mind. It made her a bit angry, but also relieved to realize that he no longer thought of her in that way.

"We are not all masters of our fate," she said. "But what about you? Except in your gardens, you do not seem to be any happier at Caradoc Court than I. Why do you stay?"

He laughed. "Right now my main reason is curiosity."

"Curiosity about what?"

He sobered immediately. "I should not have said that. I am naturally curious to see how . . . how things turn out for you and Rolf, but it is more than mere curiosity now. I am deeply interested in your welfare."

She was touched by his seriousness and she could tell he meant every word he was saying; it was not pretense on his part. "I think it is a foregone conclusion as to how things will turn out for Sir Rolf and me," she said, somewhat sadly. "It will be exactly the way he wants it—does he not get what he wants?—and I shall hate having his children." As soon as the words were out, she blushed at her audacity in mentioning such a thing to Edward.

He took her hand and said, "Oh, Jocelyn, I . . ." He broke off and dropped her hand.

"Yes? What were you going to say?"

"No matter. Listen, did you hear a rumble of thunder?" He changed the subject abruptly and looked toward the skies.

"No, but . . ." She looked up also. "Mercy, it is going to pour!" They had been so engrossed in conversation that neither of them had noticed the approaching storm.

Edward cracked the reins over the backs of the grays. "We are still a long way from the village, but there is an inn near here. Perhaps we can get there before the rain starts." But even as he said it, large drops began to splash on the carriage. By the time he stopped the horses in front of The Cloak and Candle Inn, the rain was falling steadily. He gave the reins to a boy and said, "We shall want the carriage the minute the rain stops." Then he helped Jocelyn down and held the door of the inn open for her.

Her clothing was slightly damp, but not wet, and as the day was warm, the dampness did not bother her. She looked around the large room they had entered. The walls were heavy wood paneling and exposed beams at the ceiling. On one wall were crossed swords over a coat of arms. The other walls were bare. There were approximately a dozen tables in the room, and near a stairway leading to the second story was a desk. Except for the tavern maid, no other people were in the room.

She had stopped at this same inn the day she and Gerard and Irva had gone to Caradoc Court, her wedding day, but she had gone immediately to one of the upstairs rooms to refresh herself, and tea had been brought to her there, so she had taken no notice of this big room at that time.

Edward seated her at a table and motioned to the tavern maid. "What would you like?" he asked. "The storm is likely to last for a while, so we may as well be comfortable."

"A little tea, perhaps," she said, "and some biscuits." She discovered suddenly that she was very hungry and then realized that they had both missed the midday meal.

"And I shall have a tankard of ale," Edward said. "I think we should make this a festive occasion. Would you not prefer grog to tea?"

"Oh no," Jocelyn said, surprised at his asking. "I never partake of spirits, except occasionally wine."

"Grog is only liquor much diluted by water," Edward said. "Would you like some wine, then?"

"No, tea is perfect."

The tavern maid smiled an all-knowing smile at them and left the room. Edward grinned at Jocelyn. "It is easy to read her thoughts," he said.

"Is it? I have no idea what she was thinking."

"Then I shall tell you. She thinks we are lovers who have chosen this as a trysting place."

"Oh no!" Jocelyn exclaimed, appalled. "How could she possibly think such a thing?"

"Because we are here in the middle of the day, in the middle of a storm and because . . ." he hesitated, then went on, "because we have that sly look about us."

Jocelyn could feel the blush that was stealing up from her neck to her face. She looked down at the table, too embarrassed to meet Edward's eyes. "Surely not," was all she could manage to say.

Edward laughed and made no reply.

Jocelyn felt her flushed face deepening in color, not because of Edward, but because of her thoughts. At that moment, she very much wished that what the tavern maid was thinking were true. If only she and Edward were lovers, meeting here . . . and there were no Caradoc Court and hateful husband for her to go home to.

Since she had told him the true story of her marriage to his brother she had felt, in a strange way, comforted by his presence and concern for her. Now she was suddenly light-headed, approaching a state of euphoria, and she asked herself the question: Are you not becoming much too fond of him?

That brought her back to earth quickly. She was only too well aware that she could not, under any circumstances, allow herself to become too dependent upon Edward for her few moments of happiness. She could not become fond of him, except in a sisterly way. He was her husband's brother, and she must keep that foremost in her mind.

When their repast was set before them—the maid had brought a proper tea—they fell upon the food hungrily and did not speak again until Jocelyn was drinking her second cup of tea while Edward sipped his ale.

"I am glad we are the only ones here," she said, then added hastily lest he misinterpret her words, "It is very restful and quiet."

"Also, there is no one else here, except for the tavern maid, to guess our motive in being here." Edward seemed to be laughing at her—or was he teasing her? She could not be sure, but she returned his smile. For the moment, at least, she was perfectly content. She could think of no place she would rather be, and no one whose company she would enjoy more. Caradoc Court and its master seemed very far away, both in time and distance. If only it and he could remain that way.

"What is wrong?" Edward asked.

"Why would you suppose anything is wrong?"

"Such a big sigh, as though you have more trouble than you can say grace over."

She laughed at the expression. "I was not aware that I sighed, but all things considered, perhaps I do have more than enough trouble."

"At any rate, it is good to see you laugh," he said. "It is a sight I do not see often . . . not nearly often enough."

A man came down the stairs and stopped at the desk. He looked at something on the desk and seemed about to sit down when he looked across the room and noticed the two people sitting at the table by the window. Jocelyn and Edward looked up at the man at the same time he saw them. The man nodded pleasantly, started across the room as though to speak to them, then apparently changed his mind when he was half way. "Rowena!" he called. "Where are you?"

The tavern maid came in from what was obviously the kitchen. "Yes, sir?"

"See to the lady and gentleman," the man said, then went quickly out the front door.

"Did you want something else?" the maid asked them.

"No, thank you," Edward said. "Was that the inn-keeper?"

"Yes, sir. Mr. Thaddeus Jonas. He came here about a year ago."

"He looks familiar," Edward said. "It has been more than a year since I was in here, but I could swear I have seen him before."

"He took over from his uncle," the maid said, "and he bears a close resemblance to his uncle."

"I suppose that is it, then," Edward said.

"I thought he looked familiar also," Jocelyn said when the maid left them. "I am positive I have seen him before, but I cannot imagine where."

Edward was looking out the window. "The rain seems to have stopped," he said, almost sorrowfully. "I suppose we should be on our way."

Now, for the first time, the full impact of what she had done hit Jocelyn full force, and she began to tremble. She had deliberately disobeyed Sir Rolf and come out riding with Edward. In addition, she had not appeared in his room for her hour in the late morning, and it was certain she would be late for her afternoon hour.

"What shall we say to him?" she asked Edward as the boy in front of the inn helped them both into the carriage and then grinned widely when he looked at the coin Edward pressed into his hand.

"I suppose we shall have to face the consequences of

a pleasant afternoon," Edward said, not answering her question. "For myself, I do not care, but his mistreatment of you arouses my anger as nothing else ever has. Perhaps he has not noted our absence yet," he said half-heartedly, as though he knew this was not possible.

"I am sure he has," Jocelyn said grimly. "I am supposed to go to him for an hour every morning and every afternoon. I did not go at all this morning, because I went for a long walk instead. And now I shall be late this afternoon."

She said nothing else on the ride back to Caradoc Court, and although she knew Edward was keeping up a steady prattle to distract her from worrying, she did not hear a word he said.

They left the carriage at the carriage house and returned together to the house, but no sooner were they in the courtyard than John appeared, a worried look upon his face. "Mr. Edward, Sir Rolf wants to see you and Mrs. Caradoc in his room."

"I suppose we should brace ourselves," Edward said to Jocelyn, "but do not worry. I shall take the blame for our little outing. Just leave the talking to me."

"Gladly," she said lightly in an attempt to keep him from knowing how terrified she really was.

They stopped outside Sir Rolf's door for just a minute and looked at each other. If the situation were not so unpleasant, it would be amusing, Jocelyn thought. It seemed to her preposterous that two adults were about to be admonished like children for what, at most, was a negligible offense. But when Edward briefly squeezed her hand as if to say, "Have courage. I am with you," it came to her at once how really serious the situation was. Her husband probably would be in the worst temper she had yet witnessed.

Her surmise was not mistaken. As soon as they were inside the room, she knew that Sir Rolf was too angry even to speak. His complexion, always a bit mottled, had taken on a reddish-purple hue, and a large purple vein in his temple was throbbing. He glared at his wife and brother through eyes that were narrowed to slits.

Edward was the first to speak. "Well, Rolf, you look to be in some pain. I hope you have not taken a turn for the worse. It would be a pity for you to have another relapse."

Sir Rolf opened his mouth and a choking sound came out. He sputtered for a moment, then said, "You . . . you . . ." He hesitated as though trying to think of an epithet bad enough to fling at them.

"I think you should remain calm," Edward said. "Your agitation is not helping your condition."

The irate man finally found his voice. "My condition, as you call it, was brought on entirely by two ingrates who do not have the sense to know when they are well off. I shall address myself to you first, Edward, and then you may go as I wish to speak to my wife in private."

"As you like," Edward said agreeably, "but I warn you to be careful in what you say, especially to Jocelyn. I should not like to have my wrath aroused by any foolish insinuations on your part. First, I shall tell you that Jocelyn and I went for a ride. It was entirely my idea. I thought she needed to get out for a little bit since she has been staying so close to the house of late. We were caught in a rainstorm and had to take shelter until it was over. That is why we were late in returning. Now, what is it you want to say?"

"I warned you earlier, if you remember," Sir Rolf said. "I shall not go into that again. I will tell you now, in front of my wife, that you and she are never to see each other again. You are to pack your things, Edward, and leave by nightfall. And you are never to set foot upon Caradoc soil again."

Edward stared at his brother in disbelief, then gave a short, bitter laugh. "You have truly taken leave of your senses, Rolf," he said. "In the first place, you cannot force me to leave. Our father's will settled that issue before it ever came up. I am to have a place here as long as I care to stay. And, to put it to you very explicitly, I have no intention whatever of leaving at any time in the immediate future. For that matter, I may not *ever* leave, but you may rest assured that if I do, it will be because *I* want to, not because it is your wish." Edward took a breath, then went on. "In case you have not considered this, let me remind you that should I leave Caradoc Court, the entire estate would go to rack and ruin. You know as little about management and upkeep as a child of two." He laughed again, adding, "I shudder to think what would happen to house, grounds, and farmland if they were left to your care."

Sir Rolf stared at his brother, unmistakable hatred in his eyes. But he apparently recognized the truth of what Edward had said, for instead of raging out, as both Edward and Jocelyn expected, he said in a hissing whisper, "Get out of my room! And if you so much as look at my wife again, I shall kill you."

"You are a suspicious, jealous fool, Rolf, and you have no cause . . ." Edward began.

"Get out!" This time Sir Rolf shouted. "And if you know what is good for you, you will heed what I have said."

Jocelyn started to leave with Edward when Sir Rolf shouted again, "Not you, my pretty. I have not finished with you yet."

Edward turned. "I think you should wait until you are calmer," he said. "Jocelyn can come back then."

The reddish-purple face turned an even darker color as Sir Rolf began pushing himself up from the bed. "I shall kill you right now! I shall . . ."

Edward went to the bed and pushed his brother back to the pillows. At the same time Jocelyn said, "It does not matter, Edward. I shall stay now."

When Edward left, she moved closer to the bed. Before Sir Rolf could speak, she said, "Your insane jealousy is going to make you sicker than you already are and delay your recovery further. This entire situation is really quite simple. It is just as Edward said, but the silly interpretation you have put upon it . . ."

"Woman, are you calling your husband silly?"

She looked at him steadily, then said softly, "Yes, I am. If you think there is anything at all between Edward and me other than mere civility, then you are quite the silliest person I have ever known."

He was silent for a moment, then he said, "In that case, it should cause you no hardship to learn that the two of you are not to be together again, either alone or in the company of others. Caradoc Court is large enough so that your paths need never cross. If, by accident they should, you are both to go on your way without so much as a word or a glance. Is that understood?"

She looked at him without answering.

"I shall have the servants inform me if either of you tries to go against my wishes in this and I warn you now, it will go hard with you. With both of you."

She left the room, knowing there was no point in trying to reason with him now, no point in even answering him. It was not until she was outside in the hall that she realized she was trembling violently.

"What did he say to upset you so?"

She looked up. Edward had waited outside the door for her.

"Just what he told you, only worded a bit differently," she said. "That we are not to see or speak to each other again. If we meet by accident we are to hurry along without glancing at each other."

"He is worse than a fool," Edward said. "He is an idiot."

"Idiot or not, he meant it," Jocelyn said. "He is going to have the servants report on us."

Edward sighed. "At least he did not keep you very long. I was afraid he would pour abuse on you for hours. I waited here so I could go back in and distract him if he became too unpleasant to you."

Jocelyn was suddenly so tired that it became an effort even to stand. "I must go to my room now. I am feeling a little faint."

"I should not wonder," Edward said. "Shall I have the cook prepare a tray for you?"

"No, I am not hungry in the least," she said. "All I want is some rest."

"Do not worry too much about the things Rolf says. His memory is not as long as his temper."

"Nothing is," Jocelyn said. "Oh, did I say that I enjoyed the ride, Edward, and having tea at the inn?"

"We shall do it again. Never fear, there will be other rides, other teas." With that, he left her.

How? she wondered as she went into her apartment. How could he possibly think they could manage another ride together when they were not even allowed to speak?

She sat down in the nearest chair to wait for Irva to come to help her undress. So overcome by fatigue was she that she felt unable to raise her hands above her head.

The whole day, now that she thought of it, had been peculiar, ridiculously peculiar. First, the walk into the woods, the talk with Maeve, and secondly, the ride with Edward . . .

She had meant it sincerely when she told him she had enjoyed the ride. She had enjoyed his company even more. As she had earlier in the day, she began to think about how dependent she had become upon him for the few pleasant moments in her life. But that was in the past, for now she had been denied even that.

She thought again of her state of euphoria at the inn, the feeling of quiet delight they had shared companionably, laughing to themselves at what the maid and the innkeeper probably thought about them.

The innkeeper . . .

She saw him again clearly in her mind and again she wondered why he had appeared so familiar to her, almost as though he were someone she had seen quite recently . . .

Of course! That was it! She had seen him recently . . . well, fairly recently . . . at her wedding. He was the vicar who had performed the marriage ceremony. She had not recognized him without his robes!

Eleven

In spite of her great fatigue, Jocelyn slept poorly that night, constantly rolling from one side of the big bed to the other as question after question went through her mind. A vicar was also an innkeeper? Highly unlikely, if not impossible. Then why had the vicar posed as an innkeeper? Was he also under orders from her husband to spy on her and Edward and report everything he saw back to Sir Rolf? No, that could not be, for Sir Rolf certainly had no idea that she and Edward would be out riding together that day; she herself had not even known until she returned from her walk in the woods. And even she and Edward had not known that a rainstorm would force them to seek refuge at The Cloak and Candle.

The more she thought, the more questions came into her mind—all without answers—and the more frustrated and restless she became.

Finally, in the early hours of morning, she dropped into a light sleep, and when she awoke with a start for no apparent reason, it was still early morning.

My nerves are on edge, she thought, and I shall never be able to go through breakfast with Sir Rolf this morning. What I would not give if I had never heard that name, never seen or heard . . .

But if I had never seen nor heard of Sir Rolf, I would also never have met Edward.

This thought left her so thoroughly confused as to what she really thought about anything that she decided to get up and dress.

Only one thing was clear in her mind: Somehow she had to see and talk to Edward. She had to get the information to him that the innkeeper and the vicar were the same person. It was possible that there was some reasonable explanation for this double identity and that Edward would know and could set her mind at rest. But how could she talk to him without any of the servants seeing her and reporting to Sir Rolf?

She remembered having seen his bedroom in the east wing. She certainly could not go there, but perhaps, like her, he could not sleep and had decided to work. In that case, she might find him in the little office just down the hall from his bedroom.

She had guessed correctly, and she found him seated behind the desk looking over some ledgers.

"You are at work early," she said, greeting him.

He looked up, surprised, then jumped up. "Why, good--morning." He spoke rather loudly, and she put her finger to her lips.

"We must be quiet," she said. "You do not seem to be afraid of your brother's threats, but I assure you I am. First, I was in fear for my brother's life, now I am in fear for yours also."

He looked at her curiously, then said, "Obviously you are not too much afraid or you would not be here."

"There is something I must tell you." She looked around, then closed the door of his office. "Yesterday, we both thought we had seen the innkeeper before . . ."

"Thaddeus Jonas," Edward said. "I may have seen him

before somewhere, but we were never introduced. I would have remembered that name."

"You have been introduced, but by another name. John Bedwain. He was the vicar who married your brother and me."

Edward snapped his fingers. "By Jove, you are absolutely right! He was indeed." Then a look of incredulity spread over his face. "But what goes on here? By what license does an innkeeper perform a marriage?"

"I was wondering why a vicar would pose as an innkeeper," Jocelyn said. "But, of course, you're right. It must be the other way around. The innkeeper posed as a vicar. Why?"

"That is something we are going to find out," Edward said emphatically, "and we are going to find out before this day is over." He was thoughtful for a minute. "Yesterday, when he started toward our table, he recognized us and left immediately. That means we are not supposed to find out anything. I suggest that we go back to the inn as soon as you have your morning hour with Rolf. We will question Mr. Thaddeus Jonas together and see what he has to say."

"Oh, no!" She drew back. "Sir Rolf would kill us both if we went out together today. And there is no way we can keep him from finding out."

"I have an idea that what *we* find out may soften Rolf's behaviour a great deal toward us both," Edward said slowly. "And even if we find out very little or even nothing from Jonas, it might be interesting to confront Rolf with the question of why an innkeeper performed his marriage ceremony."

She nodded and her heartbeat accelerated as she thought a little about the possible danger—but more about being with Edward again so soon after thinking she would never again have the opportunity. "Shall I meet you at the carriage house?" she asked.

"Yes, and today we shall be back in plenty of time for your afternoon hour with Rolf, so you need have no fear on that score," he said.

Jocelyn felt, during her morning hour with Sir Rolf, that she must have a look of guilt on her face for, although her husband made no comment along that line, he kept looking at her speculatively. She was not sure, however, why she should feel guilty. She had seen and talked with Edward, yes; but certainly there was nothing wrong with doing either. Perhaps, she thought, furtive would be a better word than guilty, for she did most assuredly feel furtive in what she was about to do.

She was going off in the carriage again with Edward less than twenty-hour hours after her husband had expressly forbidden her even to speak to her brother-in-law.

As usual, she said little during the hour. Sir Rolf was a talker, apparently liking the sound of his own voice and seldom calling upon her for an answer or even a comment. Consequently, she hardly ever listened to what he was saying, finding it better to concentrate on something else in order to remain in a fairly pleasant frame of mind.

This morning, though, she could think of nothing except the vicar-innkeeper. It was all she could do to keep from interrupting Sir Rolf's monologue and asking questions about the mystery that had kept her awake most of the night, but her good judgment told her it was better to remain silent, to wait at least until she and Edward could find answers to the many questions in both their minds.

". . . is that not a fact?"

She caught the last words and realized that she had been asked a question by Sir Rolf.

"What is that?" she asked.

He brought his fist down on the bed as though he were plumping a pillow. "You never listen to me," he accused. "Sometimes I get the impression that I am talking to myself."

"Then you are, at the same time, talking to an intelligent man and listening to an intelligent man talk." She would do or say almost anything to keep him from reverting to his mood of yesterday.

He laughed, long and loudly, at her words. "Damme, but you have a bit of wit," he said. "Why is it you never showed it before?"

She was about to say, "Because I have been too busy listening to false and odious accusations," but decided that such a remark would only cause her to lose ground. She smiled demurely and said nothing.

He pulled himself up to a sitting position, dangling his feet over the side of the bed, his nightshirt hanging around his ankles. "Ah, if only I could get up and walk about instead of hobble," he said. "But soon. Soon I shall be as good as ever. Here, help me to the chair."

"Are you sure you should try to walk?" she asked.

"I am perfectly capable of walking, with a little help," he said. "You may have injured me, but you did not make me a complete invalid."

She could almost see his good mood disintegrating before her eyes. She went to the bedside and held out her hand.

"Not that way! Put your right arm under my arm to support me!"

She did as she was told, and as they made their way slowly from bed to chair, it dawned upon her that they were practically in an embrace. The thought completely repelled her.

The same thought apparently struck him at that time,

for he immediately put his arm around her waist and chuckled. "Yes, my pretty, it will not be long now," he said softly.

She helped him into the chair and then drew back, her revulsion to him so strong that she actually felt ill.

"Where are you going?" he asked. "Your hour is not yet up. Are you in such a hurry to get away from me?"

"I was not leaving," she said, going to the bed. "I was only getting this pillow for your back."

"Ah, yes," he murmured as she placed the pillow behind him. "I think I am finally succeeding in taming the shrew."

She was about to flare up, tell him exactly what she thought of him, but once again her better judgment told her to remain silent. She did not want to do anything that would keep her from being able to go with Edward back to The Cloak and Candle.

She went to the window and looked out to be sure that he could not see the carriage leaving the grounds, and was gratified to see that the chapel, that afterthought of Sir Rolf's, completely obscured the view of the long tree-lined avenue leading to Caradoc Court from the highway.

"I think I should go now," she said. "My abigail is making a dress for me and I have just time for a fitting before dinner."

"There is a seamstress here," he said. "Why is your abigail sewing for you."

"She always has," Jocelyn said. "She likes to sew and seems to enjoy making my clothes."

"In the future, Maeve will make your dresses. I shall send for her this afternoon so you may meet her."

"I have met her," Jocelyn reminded him. "We stayed the night at her cottage on . . . on the night you were hurt."

His eyes narrowed as he looked at her, and she expected him to go off on a tangent, again berating her and blaming her for all of his ills and misfortune. However, he surprised her by saying only, "So we did. I had forgotten." He gave a slight smile. "It is easy to forget Maeve."

She decided he had no more wish than she to resume yesterday's unpleasantness. "I shall see you, then, this afternoon," she said, and made for the door hastily before he could call her back.

She and Edward did not try to make conversation during their ride to The Cloak and Candle. They met, again like conspirators, at the carriage house, and as the pair of grays started down the avenue, Edward snapped the reins over their backs and kept them going apace.

This time, Jocelyn thought, they really *were* conspirators. She glanced at Edward, ready to smile, but he was looking straight ahead, his brow furrowed as it usually was when he was in deep concentration. She would have given much to know what his thoughts were at that moment and, probably, if she asked, he would tell her, but she had no intention of interrupting his train of thought.

Her own thoughts seemed to float about, lighting here, there, and yonder, like puffy clouds on a lazy, sunny day. Mostly she thought about Edward, about how much she enjoyed his company, his closeness now, the security she felt with him, the likes and dislikes they had in common.

She changed her thoughts abruptly, knowing that she was on dangerous ground. She could not afford to sort out or analyze her thoughts about Edward for fear of what might be revealed to her. She could not admit, even to herself, how she felt about him. The one thought which must remain in her mind at all times was that Edward was her husband's brother. He would always be her brother-in-law. That, and nothing more.

The same young boy they had seen yesterday was standing in front of The Cloak and Candle as they alighted from the carriage, and his face brightened as he recognized Edward.

" 'Day to ye, sir," he said, jumping to take the reins. "When might you be wanting 'er back?"

"Only a few minutes at most," Edward said. "No need to unhitch the pair."

"We may have a bit of trouble getting the innkeeper to see us," Edward said as he held the door open for her. "Especially if he is not in the tavern part and we have to send for him."

But they were in luck. Thaddeus Jonas was seated behind the desk near the entrance to the large room, apparently making entries in a large ledger. He did not look up until Edward and Jocelyn stood directly in front of him and Edward said, "Mr. Jonas?"

The man looked up and started visibly when he saw the couple. "Ye–es, what can I do for you?"

"I believe you know who we are," Edward said, "but I shall refresh your memory in case it is not as long as ours. I am Edward Caradoc, and this is my sister-in-law, Mrs. Rolf Caradoc."

The innkeeper held out his hand. "I do not believe I have had the pleasure. I surely would have remembered."

"There is no need for you to keep up this pretense with us," Edward said. "You were first introduced to us as John Bedwain, the vicar who performed the marriage ceremony for my brother and his wife. Obviously, you are not a vicar. I want to know only one thing: Why were you posing as one?"

The man's face had gone ashen as Edward talked, and now he looked as though he might faint. His eyes kept darting from Edward to Jocelyn as though he expected some harm to come to him from one of them, but was not sure which one would move toward him first. Had the situation not been so serious, Jocelyn would have found it amusing to view such extreme, yet deserved, discomfiture.

"I—I . . . haven't the slightest idea what you are talking about," Thaddeus stuttered. "I am an innkeeper. I know nothing about any vicar or any wedding." Then regaining some of his composure, he continued, "Obviously a case of mistaken identity, sir."

Edward said nothing, but he took a step forward, then sidewise, as though he was going behind the desk.

"Do you have a twin brother?" Jocelyn asked suddenly.

"N—no, ma'am."

"I thought not," she said. "There is no doubt at all that you are the one."

"No, no, there is some error . . ." he began, but Edward stopped him in midsentence with a look.

"If you are not the one, then you will not mind at all returning with us to Caradoc Court and facing my brother," Edward said easily. "Then if you both can convince us that you are not the one, Mrs. Caradoc and I shall pursue this no further."

Thaddeus Jonas began to tremble. "I cannot leave the inn," he said. "Impossible! There is no one here but me."

This was not meant to be the innkeeper's most fortunate day, for he had no sooner finished speaking than the door to the kitchen opened, and Rowena, the maid who had waited upon them yesterday, came in.

Jocelyn, in spite of herself, began to laugh, and Edward smiled broadly. "Come," he said, "the sooner we go, the sooner you may return to your business."

"No—wait," the innkeeper said. He looked around the room as though he expected deliverance from some unseen source, and when none came, he said, "There is no need for me to go to Caradoc Court."

"Then you will tell us what we want to know here and now," Edward said.

The man bowed his head and said softly, "Sir Rolf paid me to pose as a vicar and perform the ceremony. Paid me handsomely."

"Why?" Jocelyn beat Edward to the question. "Why did he do that?"

"You must believe me," Thaddeus Jonas said earnestly, "if I knew, I would tell you, but I would not even know how to guess his reason."

Edward and Jocelyn looked at each other in bewilderment. They both knew that Thaddeus Jonas was—at last —telling them the truth and that he could not answer the biggest question of all: Why had Rolf paid this man to pose as a vicar to perform the marriage ceremony when he could just as easily have gotten the real vicar from the village?

Seeing no need to ask any more questions, they left The Cloak and Candle. The ride back to Caradoc Court was anything but silent. At times in the conversation, Edward and Jocelyn interrupted each other, at other times, they talked simultaneously, each speculating, each guessing, each trying to make some sense out of something that made no sense at all.

"At least, you are back in good time," Edward said as they turned from the highway into the avenue.

"Yes," she said, "I have a good two hours before I have to go to his room."

At the carriage house, Edward said, "I am going to the stables to get Regent, my horse, and ride to the county seat. It will be quicker than taking the carriage."

"But why?" Jocelyn asked, surprised. "Surely you are not going to try to have the innkeeper arrested? You would be getting your brother in trouble as well and," she paled at the thought of it, "and I also since I was a party to it all, albeit an unknowing party."

Edward patted her shoulder. "Have no worry on that score. I have no intention of seeing the police. I do have business at the county seat, however, and I will tell you about it when I return." He rushed toward the stables as though the more he thought about his errand, the more in haste he was.

Jocelyn watched until she saw him go by the carriage house on Regent at a full gallop, then she went back to her apartment in the house. For a long time she sat in her bedroom, her mind still going over again and again the conversation with the innkeeper. The same questions kept coming up, and she was no nearer to an answer than she had been with Edward.

Why? Why had Sir Rolf paid an innkeeper to impersonate a vicar to perform the marriage ceremony? *Paid me handsomely*, the innkeeper had said. So it must have meant a great deal to Sir Rolf.

She got up and started toward the door. There was one way to get an answer to her question, and that was to ask Sir Rolf, of course. See him face to face and come right out with it. He would have to give her some kind of answer, and, just possibly, her knowledge of the peculiar affair might surprise the truth out of him.

But she stopped at the door. It would be better, she thought, to wait for Edward. It would at least be better for him to know that she was confronting her husband, whether or not Edward was with her when she did it.

She sat down again, resting her head against the back of the chair, and stared up at the evil grin on the ugly gargoyle.

There was a light rap at her door only a few minutes

before the time for her to go to Sir Rolf. Thinking he probably had sent John for her, she frowned as she opened the door.

Edward stood before her, a look on his face which she could not interpret, a look which was a mixture of bewilderment, pleasure, excitement . . . and, maybe, anticipation.

Without speaking, he stepped into her small sitting room and closed the door, then he put his arms around her. More in surprise than alarm, she drew away from him. For a minute he looked at her, smiling broadly, then he said, "I have news."

"What is it?" she asked. "What was your errand at the county seat?"

"As we were coming back from the inn, it occurred to me that a marriage performed by Thaddeus Jonas might not be a valid marriage," Edward said, "so I went to the county seat and looked in the Book of Records." He paused, a twinkle coming into his eye.

"Yes?" Jocelyn said, her heart beginning to race.

"No marriage between Jocelyn Egmont and Sir Rolf Caradoc has been recorded."

She stared at him, not understanding fully. When she made no comment, Edward said, "So—there is no legal and binding marriage between you."

Still she stared at him, unable to take in this momentous news, this strange development.

Edward's smile turned into a laugh, and he took her in his arms again, this time tilting her face up and kissing her. "You, my dear sister-in-law, are not my sister-in-law at all. You are my love."

Helen Taylor

or the first few days to get to the door. Thirteen ... weeks
story had sent Edna for her. She frowned as she went into ...
Matron.

Twelve

Jocelyn awoke the next morning feeling light-headed,
almost giddy. It took her a few minutes to remember why,
and when she did, she bounded out of bed and rang for
her breakfast. When Irva appeared, Jocelyn sang out
"Good-morning" with a lilt that had been missing from
her voice for a long time. Irva, noticing, looked at her
in surprise. "Good-morning, miss."

"Today is the most beautiful day I have seen since
I came here," Jocelyn said.

"Oh, no, miss!" Irva looked at her as though she had
lost her senses. "It is raining." She pulled the draperies
aside so that Jocelyn could see.

"No matter," Jocelyn said. "It is a beautiful day." She
wanted to tell Irva the good news, but she decided she
had better wait until she and Edward talked further about
his findings—or rather, what he had not found—at the
county seat yesterday. They had not had a chance to talk
the day before because it was time for her hour with Sir
Rolf shortly after Edward's return, and then, after supper,
Edward had had to speak to a new tenant who was going
to farm some of the land belonging to Caradoc Court.

She and Edward had agreed just before she went in
to Sir Rolf that neither of them would mention what they

had found out at the inn or what he had found missing in the records at the county seat until they had had a chance to discuss it at greater length.

As soon as Jocelyn finished her breakfast, she went to the east wing, looking for Edward. As she suspected, he was in his office.

"Good-morning, my love," Edward greeted her, rising from his desk immediately and kissing her. "I have never seen you looking more beautiful—or more carefree!" He laughed, as though it was impossible to contain his own good humor.

Jocelyn's heart soared. It would have been enough happiness to fill her to the brim for the rest of her life just to learn that she was not married to Sir Rolf, but to find out at the same time that Edward loved her, and to discover that the feelings for him which she had been trying to suppress were, indeed, love also, made her happiness spill over. How was it possible that in such a short space of time, everything had turned completely around? She had thought she would have to spend the rest of her life chained to a man she loathed. Instead, she was free now, free to express her feelings for Edward, feelings which had undergone a radical change.

She laughed as she said, "It is hard to believe that just a short time ago I disliked you intensely."

"Or that I distrusted both you and your motives," Edward said. "And yet, even so, I knew I was still immensely attracted to you." He pulled a chair up to his desk for her, saying, "But right now, I think we must discuss this strange business before we can get to more personal matters."

"Yes," she agreed, "I am still very much in the dark as to what has been going on and, for that matter, why it has been going on."

"And I," Edward admitted. "I stayed awake most of the night trying to understand why Rolf did what he did. It was common knowledge all over the countryside that he wanted to get married—has wanted to for years. And I know for a fact that he was extremely pleased when . . . an arrangement was made for him to marry you. Extremely pleased is hardly emphatic enough; he was beside himself with joy. I have not seen Rolf in such a good mood for years. So why did he behave as he did? Why did he . . ." He broke off, his puzzled expression giving way to one of complete bewilderment.

Jocelyn shook her head. "I cannot imagine! None of it makes any sense at all to me."

As though by recounting the odd events he could clarify them, Edward said, "First, he does not make the marriage legal in the county, then he hires someone to pose as a vicar. And yet he lets you, and everyone else, believe that it is a legal and binding marriage. How long would he have gone on with this pretense?"

"I think probably forever," she said. "He does not strike me as being the kind to admit to wrongdoing of any kind."

"You are quite right."

"I am wondering what he will say when we confront him with what we know," Jocelyn said.

Edward was about to speak, then he paused for several minutes, thinking. Jocelyn watched him, wondering if she would ever be able to read his mind, to know what he was thinking. She felt that one only had to look at her to know what she was thinking right now, for she was sure her love for Edward was as clear on her face as though it were written there with indelible ink.

"I think," Edward said finally, "that we should go on exactly as we have been—at least for a few days—until we find out the reason behind Rolf's actions. If we let him know now, it may give him an advantage unless we know the *why* of it all."

"But how can we find out why unless we ask him?" she asked.

"I doubt if we could find out by asking him," Edward said. "It is not likely that he would tell us the truth."

"You are right," she said. "But I have not the slightest notion how to go about finding out. Have you?"

"I am going to give it a great deal of thought," he said. "Somehow, I am going to find out. I know that more than anything in the world, Rolf wanted an heir to whom he could leave Caradoc Court. The idea that I might someday be sole owner galled him as nothing else ever could."

"But why?" she asked. "You are his brother, after all."

"I have never known for certain," Edward said, "but I suppose it began when I was just a baby. I think Rolf might have been jealous of the attention my father paid me. He should have realized that, my mother having died when I was born, my father naturally would pay me more attention than he would otherwise."

"Yes, I imagine so, but it all seems terribly unfair to you," she said, bristling at the idea of anyone treating Edward so, especially a young, vulnerable Edward. She stood up. "I will leave you to your work," she said. "And it is nearly time for . . . Oh, Edward, must I still go to Sir Rolf every morning and every afternoon? I do not think I can bear it now."

"Do as you like," he said. "Think up an excuse for avoiding him, if you want, but do not let him even suspect that you know you are not his wife."

Jocelyn smiled. "All right, but I shall be happy indeed when I can say to him, 'You, sir, are not my husband, and I shall never have to take another order from you!' "

Back in her own rooms, Jocelyn decided she was in no frame of mind to see Sir Rolf this morning and, knowing that he would send for her, she left the house and went out to the gardens, hoping that John, or whoever Sir Rolf sent, would not think of looking for her outside. The rain had stopped, but there was still a fine drizzle, and surely no one would expect her to be out in it.

She went to the rose garden, her favorite, and as always it reminded her of Egmont House, and that, in turn, reminded her of Gerard. She wondered what her brother would say about this latest turn of events. Would he take her back home again, or would he insist that she go through with this farce, this pretense of being married to Sir Rolf? Knowing Gerard, she was afraid he would demand that she stay on at Caradoc Court as Sir Rolf's wife because, after all, if she left, his checks would stop.

Although she and Edward had not formally declared their love for each other, she knew it would happen very soon now. And what then? What would their future be? Certainly she could not marry Edward and remain here as his wife with Sir Rolf suddenly becoming the third party. And it was unthinkable that she remain here one minute longer than necessary. As soon as she and Edward had solved the mystery of why his brother had acted as he had, she would be on her way to Egmont House at once, no matter what Gerard said or did.

She touched a particularly large red rose and bent over to brush her face against the damp, velvety petals and to smell that pungent aroma, unlike any other. Edward's roses, on which he had spent countless hours—brushing her face against one of them was almost like a caress from Edward.

The mere thought of him caused a tingle of excitement to run through her. How much everything had changed in so short a time! Yesterday she had been in love with him, but she had had to bury her feelings so deep inside that even she had not recognized them for what they were.

How long had she been in love with Edward? Certainly not from the beginning. She thought again of that first time she had seen him, the day he went to Egmont House to take the betrothal ring—a ring which, incidentally, she had never worn. She had thought Edward rather curt and rude then, but she had not dreamed how low his opinion of her had been. Had she known that, and his reason for that opinion, she would not have thought his behavior strange in the least.

She remembered even then she had wanted a friend and ally at Caradoc Court, and had been disappointed in thinking that Edward, like his brother, would be anything but that.

And yet, in spite of his seeming rudeness even after she and Sir Rolf were "married," she had still wanted him for a friend. She knew now that the attraction had been much deeper than she knew. It was something she had feared greatly and thus had kept trying to push out of her mind as long as she had thought she was married to another man, even though she knew she would always despise her husband. Finding she was not actually married had freed her in body, mind, spirit . . . and heart. Now she could love Edward inwardly, outwardly, and openly. At least, she could as soon as the mystery was solved.

It seemed to her now that he, as well as she, was reveling in this new freedom. Since yesterday afternoon they had laughed and smiled more than they had in all the time since she came to Caradoc Court. And her mind kept going back to that moment when he had said, *"You are my love."* She would never forget the words, the tone of his voice, nor the look on his face. They were like a gift to her. In fact, at this moment, it was as though she had suddenly been given back her life itself to keep now for her very own. It belonged to her again and to no one else . . . until such time as she chose to give it to another.

How long before that would be possible? How long before she and Edward . . .

"M'lady!" The voice intruded upon her thoughts with the finality of a funeral knell. She whirled around and looked straight at John.

"I did not mean to frighten you," he said. "Sir Rolf sent me out to look for you. He wants to see you right now."

Out of habit, she took a few steps toward the house, then she stopped. "Tell Sir Rolf it is not convenient for me to see him this morning. I shall see him this afternoon . . . if I have time."

John's astonishment was evident in the way he looked at her. Then he nodded and, without a word, left her, obviously dreading to deliver such a message to Sir Rolf.

She smiled slightly, then bent down and inhaled deeply the fragrance of the large red rose.

She thought she knew what to expect when she went to Sir Rolf's room that afternoon, but she was not prepared for the violence of his temper. No sooner was she inside the door than he sat bolt upright in bed and glared at her as though she were a viper which had just crawled from beneath a rock.

"Good-afternoon," she said. "I trust you are in improved health."

"Damme, woman, if I could do so without pain to myself, I would strangle you here and now."

"I know," she replied sweetly, "therefore it is fortunate for me that you cannot do so without pain."

He stared at her now in mute rage for a moment, then

he bellowed, "Have your senses flown out the window? Are you completely mad?" So angry was he that he began to sputter and had to break off.

She sat down in the chair beside his bed and waited for the rage to diminish. All the while she was thinking, How can an adult behave so? How can anyone lose control so completely?

"Well, have you nothing to say for yourself?" Sir Rolf roared finally. "Why were you not here this morning? What do you mean by sending me an impertinent answer . . . and by a servant, at that? Speak, madam! Give an accounting of yourself at once!"

"I was enjoying the rose garden when John found me this morning," she said. "I did not feel like coming to see you at that time."

Again, he was overcome by rage. His face turned such a deep shade of purple that Jocelyn was afraid he would have an attack of some kind.

"Did you not," he began when he could talk again, "did you not, in your marriage vows, promise to love, honor and obey me?"

"Yes, I did," she said lightly.

"Is your memory so short that you cannot recollect those vows? Do I have to remind you every day?"

"To be perfectly truthful," she said, "I am finding it exceedingly hard to love one who is completely without love, and to honor one who does not know the meaning of the word honor. And as for obedience . . . Now is as good a time as any to tell you that I have no intention of spending an hour with you every morning and again every afternoon. If you want to send me back to Egmont House for my disobedience, that will be fine with me . . ."

"Ah, I see your little game now," he interrupted. "Odd that it did not occur to me earlier." He began to laugh his unpleasant laugh. "You think you can taunt and annoy me until I send you away. Well, you are very much mistaken, my pretty. You are my wife, and if that fact is not known to you now, it certainly will be as soon as I am able to get out of this bed again! And, you are forgetting something entirely in plotting your bold little plan. You are forgetting your brother. Does the state of his health not bother you?"

"Gerard was in good health when last I saw him," she said, "and I see no reason why he should not remain in good health for some time to come."

"Do not be too sure of that. That is another score I can settle easily once I am well again."

She ignored his threats. "As I was saying, I shall not be spending very much time with you in the future. I may come in early to bid you a brief good-morning, but it is unlikely that you will see me again during the day."

It was obvious he could not believe his ears. "What is the matter? What has happened to you?" He was almost screaming the words at her.

"Why, nothing at all, sir," she said. "It is merely that I find a sickroom too dreary a place for a newlywed." With that, she left the room before he could say another word.

Thirteen

A day passed, and then another and another, and each day left Jocelyn more perplexed than the one before. There were too many factors in what she and Edward referred to as "their mystery" that, instead of becoming clearer, had become even more confusing. The more they tried to find a reason for Sir Rolf's strange actions, the less likely it seemed that they would without asking Sir Rolf himself point-blank, and they both knew that his answer would be nowhere near the truth.

The chief reason for Jocelyn's confusion, however, was not lack of a reason for Sir Rolf's actions, but Edward's current actions. True, Edward was both tender and solicitous toward her and with every glance told her that he loved her. But Jocelyn was enormously concerned because he had never put his feeling into words. With the exception of "You are my love" on that first afternoon of the "discovery," not another word of love had passed his lips. Also, he had made no reference whatever to any future that they might have together.

Thinking she could bring matters to a head and elicit a formal declaration from him of both his love for her and his intentions for the future, she said to him on the fourth day after their visit with Thaddeus Jonas, "Ed-

175

ward, I have been thinking that since I am not Sir Rolf's wife, I should go back to Egmont House. It does not seem quite proper for me to stay here, unchaperoned at that."

He gave her an odd look and did not reply for a minute or two. When he spoke, it was only to say, "I think you should remain, at least until we clear up this matter."

That, of course, told her nothing. She had wanted him to implore her to stay because he could not do without her; she had wanted him to end his declaration of love with a formal proposal of marriage.

Disappointed beyond words, she had left him and gone to her little sitting room to ponder the whole situation and arrive at some idea of what she should do now. It was becoming increasingly obvious that she and Edward were not going to find out Sir Rolf's motives—and that Edward was going to make no overtures toward her until they did. Her initial relief in finding she was not married after all was beginning to be almost overshadowed by her new worry.

As she sat in the small room, inadvertently glancing up now and then at the grinning gargoyle, she thought suddenly of Maeve McCaulay. On the morning when she had walked through the woods and talked with Maeve, the woman had said that all was not as it should be at Caradoc Court and had suggested that Jocelyn visit the Caradoc family graves beneath the chapel. In the excitement of all that she had learned since then, Jocelyn had completely forgotten Maeve and her strange insinuations.

She went at once to the chapel and on entering stopped dead still. She had not returned to this place since the day of her "wedding," and seeing it now brought back all of the terrible, depressing feelings she had had that day. The chapel was not nearly as large as it had seemed then.

It was, in fact, rather small. There were five rows of pews on each side of a center aisle which led to the altar. The aisle, which had seemed so long when she had walked in with Gerard and out with Sir Rolf, was actually no distance at all!

She gave a huge sigh and tried to push the unpleasant memories aside. Going down the aisle now, she noticed for the first time the small stairway beside the altar. Those were, no doubt, the steps which led to the graves below, as Maeve had said.

She started down, then realized that she would need a light, for it was very dark at the bottom of the stairway. Just as she was about to go outside to ask for a lantern, she saw one hanging beside the door. She lighted it and started back down the narrow staircase.

Even with the lantern, she had to blink her eyes several times to become accustomed to the darkness. Although the area was not below ground, there were no windows in the massive stone walls. The room was small and had no floor except the earth, from which six flat tombstones protruded slightly.

Looking at this miniature graveyard, she suddenly had an eerie feeling of displacement. She did not belong here, nor did she want to be here with these long-dead Caradocs. Involuntarily, she began to shiver, trembling violently. Finally, when she could control herself, she started back up the stairs, but halfway, she stopped.

She had come to see what Maeve had said was not quite right and, having gone this far, she should not leave without at least seeing what was written on the stones. Obviously, there was nothing else to find out, because the graves were ordinary graves.

She went back down the stairs and began with the graves in the far corner. Sir Ronald Caradoc and his wife, Catherine, according to the inscription on the stones. Except for the names, there was nothing else but the dates of their births and deaths.

She moved to the next two graves, holding the lantern down to read the inscriptions. Sir Mallory Caradoc and his wife, Jane, and the dates of their births and deaths.

She went to the last two stones, those nearest the stairway, and again held the lantern down. Sir Charles Caradoc and his wife, Beatrice. Again, there was nothing else but birth and death dates.

Sir Charles and Lady Beatrice, of course, were the parents of Rolf and Edward—the third generation of Caradocs buried beneath the chapel—or in the family graveyard, since at the time of their burial there had been no chapel. She looked at the dates. Sir Charles was born in 1748 and died in 1798, and his wife Beatrice was born in 1753 and died in 1789.

It all seemed much longer ago than it actually was since it was in another century. She counted back from this year, 1814, to 1798, the date of Sir Charles's death . . . sixteen years. Edward had said he was eight years old when his father died, and he was twenty-four now, having been born, as he told her, in 1790.

There was nothing here to substantiate Maeve's claim that all was not as it should be at Caradoc Court. Jocelyn wondered why the woman had suggested that she look at the family graves. The six graves were much like any others, except that they had been enclosed in stone walls and had a roof—which was the floor of the chapel. She held the lantern high, surveying the entire scene. No, there was nothing out of the ordinary here.

She went again to each of the four walls to be sure she had overlooked nothing, touching the cold stone here and there. The walls were simply walls and the stone was plain graystone. Had Maeve been trying to alarm her by making her think something was wrong? Why would the woman do that? Then again, why had Maeve sent her to this enclosed burial ground, knowing she would find nothing?

Jocelyn shook her head in confusion as she started back up the narrow stairs. It was all too much for her; she could only conclude that everyone connected with Caradoc Court—herself and Edward excepted, of course —was either completely mad or, at best, distinctly odd.

At the top of the steps, she halted, thinking . . . Edward . . .

There was something in the back of her mind . . . something not quite right . . . about the dates . . .

Hurriedly she went back down the stairs. She held the lantern to the stones of Sir Charles and Beatrice and squinted at the dates for a long time. Yes, there it was. Either one of the dates was wrong . . . No, that could not be, for if the stonecutter had made a mistake, Sir Rolf would have had him correct it or else begin again on a new stone. She knew him well enough to know he would not tolerate an error of that kind, or any kind if someone other than he himself made it. So the date was correct.

Beatrice had died 19 August 1789, more than a year before Edward was born.

She remembered Edward's telling her that he had been born on the sixteenth of September in 1790.

Edward could not possibly be the son of Lady Beatrice Caradoc.

That, then, was why Maeve had sent her to the graves; that had been what the woman was referring to when she implied that all was not as it should be at Caradoc Court.

Edward himself had told her that his mother had died when he was born. Obviously, that was not true. If Beatrice was not his mother, it seemed likely that Sir

Charles was not his father. Who, then, was Edward?

These thoughts went round and round in her head. Feeling weak, she gripped the rough stone wall to steady herself. She must get out of here at once before the shock of this new discovery made her ill.

She hurried up the stairs, half falling as she bent over to replace the lantern in its accustomed corner. Scarcely aware of what she was doing or where she was going, she ran outside the chapel and headed in the direction of the rose garden.

Just as she turned the corner around the west wing of the house, she saw John hurrying to her. "M'lady," he said breathlessly, "I have been looking for you. Sir Rolf wants to see you. He said to ask you if it would be convenient for you to come to his room for a few minutes?"

Jocelyn looked at John, not quite believing the wording of the message. For the past few mornings, she had been stopping by Sir Rolf's room, going just inside the door and bidding him good-morning. Usually she added that she hoped his health was improving, that he was in no pain. She did not tarry. The longest she had stayed was three or four minutes. His first reaction to this was what she expected: a sputtering, near incoherent rage. For the past two mornings, however, he had merely looked at her and nodded, or else returned her "good-morning."

It could be, she thought, that instead of Sir Rolf's taming the shrew, she herself had begun to tame the wild beast by letting him know that he could not always have his way, that she would not be ordered around.

Or was the message John brought the epitome of sarcasm?

Nevertheless, she answered, "Yes, I shall go at once." It could be that he wanted to see her on some important matter. Perhaps he, of his own accord, was going to confess what he had done, the way he had misled—no, that was too mild a word for what he had done—the way he had lied to and deceived her about the wedding.

And, of course, now there was that other thing also. It was impossible that Sir Rolf did not know about the discrepancy in the date of Beatrice's death and Edward's birth. After all, he was eighteen years older than Edward, an adult at the time of Edward's birth, so he was well aware of . . . Of what?

Before going to Sir Rolf's room, she went to her own apartment first in order to change her dress, the one she had on having become soiled around the hem from the dirt at the graves. She wondered why Sir Rolf had never bothered to put a floor there. The tombstones could have formed part of the floor, as they did in many cathedrals and abbeys. But, knowing Sir Rolf as she had come to know him, she supposed he could not be bothered with something that would not be seen. Visitors to Caradoc Court would hardly be taken to the tiny burial ground beneath the chapel.

She decided to put on her prettiest dress, a green brocade, and to look her most fetching for Sir Rolf. Perhaps that would be a way to entice the truth out of him. She would also be as agreeable as possible.

She knocked lightly at his door and was speechless when Sir Rolf himself opened the door.

"Well, my dear, you deign to do more than pop in to wish me good-morning—finally." He was smiling at her even though there was a touch of sarcasm in his voice.

"At your request," she said.

"Ah, yes, at my request. Come in, come in. You need not just stand there gawking at me as though I were something on view at the county fair."

"I was surprised to see you up," she said. "Delighted, also, I may add."

"I have been up a good bit of the time these past few

days," he said, "which you would have known had you done more than stick your head into the doorway for a minute. Well, no matter, come in now and sit down."

Without waiting for her to be seated, he sat down in the chair beside the window. "You are such a gadabout these days, I was not sure that John would find you."

She looked at him without answering. He did look—and seem—much stronger. The little lines caused by pain had left his face, and when he had walked from the door to the chair, he had moved much faster than he had at any time since the accident. "I am glad to find you so much improved," she said finally.

"Ah, yes," he said, "every day finds me much better. I have been walking around in the room here for several days, and tomorrow I think I shall take my walk into the rest of the house. Not so confining."

She nodded, glad to know he was improving, but horrified at the thought of running into him anywhere in the house. As long as he was confined to this room, she felt a certain amount of safety, but if he began strolling through the halls . . .

"I owe you for my sudden recuperation," he interrupted her thoughts, "just as I owe you for my being here in the first place."

"How is that?" she asked.

"When you stopped coming in for our little visits, I decided that was a good enough incentive for me to hurry the mending of my back and leg. I began moving about more in the room and discovered that the more I did, the easier it became. You see, my dear, if a wife cannot take the time to visit her husband, then I think it is the husband's place to visit his wife."

She wanted to scream at him, "I am not your wife and never will be." However, she knew this would be folly. She remained quiet.

"It is only a matter of days now," he went on, "before I shall be able to leave this room—permanently. My place is with you and yours is with me, until death do us part."

She could only stare at him, mouth agape. How long was he going to go on with this madness?

"Only a little while now, and I shall be moving into that lovely apartment I prepared for us, which you now occupy all alone."

Disgust was rising in her. Was he taunting her, or could he seriously think that she wanted to share the rooms with him? Surely he could not, not after all she had done and said.

"Why was it you wanted to see me?" she asked.

"Why, indeed!" He looked at her incredulously, as though she had asked the question of a simpleton. "Why would I not want to see my wife? I have missed your visits, my dear, and, also, I wanted to share my good news with you."

"What news is that?"

Now he looked disappointed. "The good news that I am on the mend, of course, and that soon we shall be living together as man and wife. That is as it should be, naturally."

She bit her tongue, restraining herself from saying anything that would give away what she knew. It was quite obvious that he was going to say nothing that even touched on his devious, if not out-and-out illegal, behavior of the past weeks. But perhaps—just perhaps, it would be possible to get him, unwittingly, to divulge something else.

"You would never imagine where I was this morning," she said, changing the subject drastically.

"No, where were you?"

"I visited the Caradoc burial ground—under the chapel."

She waited to see what effect this would have on him,

but if it affected him at all, he did not show it.

"How did you know where to find it?" he asked. "And why were you interested in visiting it?"

"I was in the chapel," she said, "and I saw the stairway beside the altar. I wanted to see where it led." It was not a lie, at least, not completely.

"I see," he nodded. "Well, it could not have been a very amusing morning for you. There is no one buried there except my parents, grandparents, and great-grandparents."

"Yes, I saw. Were there no other children?"

"Oh, yes, plenty of them," he said heartily. "But only the eldest son and his wife are buried there—the inheritors of Caradoc Court and the title." He began laughing. "More children! My father was one of eleven and his father one of eight. And I have every reason to believe that you and I shall do just as well by the name Caradoc."

"But your father had only two: you and Edward," she said, sorely disgusted with the turn of the conversation, but determined, nevertheless, to get as much information from him as possible.

"Yes, only two, but there would have been more, had my mother lived longer."

She wanted to remind him that there was an eighteen-year gap getween his age and Edward's, but she knew it would be inappropriate to pursue the matter further, and also his suspicions might be aroused.

She arose. "I think I should be going now. I should not like to tire you too much just when you are beginning to feel so much better."

"May I expect you back this afternoon?"

"I think not. Perhaps tomorrow."

"Have you not a kiss for your husband before you go?"

This was the first time he had suggested any personal contact between them. The idea of kissing him repelled her, but in order to avoid a scene, she bent and lightly kissed him on the forehead.

He laughed. "We shall do better than that by and by," he said. "I can wait."

She left quickly. He had not mentioned Edward nor his command that she and Edward neither see each other nor speak if they met by accident. Obviously, he must have known that she and Edward had been seeing each other, for they had made no secret of the fact, nor had they tried to meet surreptitiously. Although she had her breakfast in her room every morning, she and Edward ate the midday meal together in the dining room, as well as the evening meal.

It was possible that Sir Rolf was as desirous as she of avoiding unpleasantness. He might have decided that if he were a bit nicer to her, his manner a bit more courteous, she might become a more willing bride.

It was time for dinner and so she headed for the dining room now, but just as she was about to enter, she stopped cold.

Since leaving the chapel she had been as obsessed with the question of Edward's identity as she was with Edward himself, and suddenly it came to her that the only logical explanation must be that Edward was the illegitimate son of Sir Rolf.

There was, after all, an eighteen-year difference in their ages, and it seemed entirely plausible that Rolf as a young man was no better than Rolf as an older man. He was despicable now; he could have been a wastrel then.

Good Lord! she thought, aghast. Could it be? Edward, her beloved, the by-blow of that scoundrel and . . . whom? Some maid or tavern wench who was no better than she should be?

She leaned against the wall, unable to support herself any longer. The thought was too terrible to entertain.

Surely not Edward also! Surely he would not deceive her, even as Sir Rolf had.

Yet, if Edward was indeed Rolf's son, deception might come as easy for the son as for the father.

For a moment only, she found herself despising Edward almost as much as she did Sir Rolf.

The moment passed. She could not despise someone whom she loved so much, at least not without giving him a fair hearing. She decided that the only honest thing she could do would be to tell Edward about her visit beneath the chapel this morning. Tell him she knew of the discrepancy in his birth date and the date of his "mother's" death. And then she would ask him outright if Sir Rolf was his father.

Resolutely, she pushed the door of the dining room open and went in.

Fourteen

Edward was in the dining room, having arrived just before Jocelyn, and Hugo was standing beside the table, waiting to serve the meal. Edward rose and seated Jocelyn. "Have you had a busy morning?" he asked.

"Quite," she said. "I should like to tell you about it." She paused, waiting for Hugo to serve and then discreetly withdraw.

Edward looked at her with a mildly curious expression on his face. "I did not see you anywhere about during the morning," he said.

Hugo bowed slightly and asked, "Is there anything else you would like?" and then withdrew when they both replied, "No, thank you."

"You would not have seen me," Jocelyn said, "unless you had been in the chapel."

"The chapel?" There was surprise in Edward's voice.

"Beneath the chapel, actually," she said. "I visited the family graves."

"Good Lord!" Edward exclaimed, "I would call that a fairly morbid pastime. Did you think to study family history that way?"

"That was not my thought," she said, "however, I did learn some interesting things." She waited to see what he would say, but he merely nodded and concentrated on the food on his plate, so she said, "Of most interest to me were the dates on the tombstones."

Edward looked up. "What could be interesting about the birth and death dates of my ancestors?" His attitude seemed genuine.

"Have you never looked at the dates?" she asked.

He shrugged. "Not really, I suppose. I was never one for visiting gravesites. I have not seen those graves since Rolf had the chapel built over them. Has he had something done to the tombstones?"

Could it be possible that he did not know about the discrepancy between the dates of Beatrice's death and his own birth? She had to find out some way if he was as adept at deceit as his brother.

"I was under the impression that your mother died when you were born," she said.

"She did," Edward said. "She died just a few hours after my birth, or so I was told."

"Who told you that?"

Edward was thoughtful. "I believe it was Rolf. I remember when I was very small and asked questions, my father told me that my mother had gone to live with the angels. After my father died—when I was eight—I asked more questions because the subject of death was very much on my mind then. It was Rolf, I remember, who told me then that our mother had died giving birth to me. To be more specific, the way he worded it left me believing that I was the cause of our mother's death . . . even though I do not believe he came right out and stated that I killed her. For years I felt guilty, as though I were a murderer. Then, some years ago, I learned that a number of women die in childbirth and my mother happened to be one of them. That was when I stopped considering myself a murderer, more a victim of fate—both my mother and me."

"Rolf lied to you," Jocelyn said, "deliberately and cruelly."

"What do you mean? How can you know?"

"Beatrice Caradoç died a little over a year before you were born."

"That is not possible!" Edward half rose from his seat. "There is some mistake."

"Yes," she nodded, "that was my first thought also —that there was a mistake in the date on the stone. Then I realized that the stone must have been put there shortly after her death and that, had there been a mistake, Sir Charles certainly would have had it corrected."

Edward was silent for a long time, staring down at his plate as though he expected to find a solution to everything there. Finally, he looked up. "You are sure about this?"

"Absolutely. Edward . . ." She said his name imploringly, "Edward, please do not deceive me. I do not think I could bear that from you. If you knew . . ."

Edward got up instantly and went to her. He put his arm around her shoulders, ignoring the watching eyes of Hugo. "Jocelyn, I swear to you that I knew nothing. I thought that my mother died at my birth, just as I was told. I think now . . . Oh, God, I don't know what to think now! I only know that you must believe me— believe that I am telling you the truth."

"I believe you," she said, and she did. She should have known that deceit was not part of Edward's nature and never could be, no matter who his parents were.

"I am going to Rolf immediately and demand the truth from him," Edward said, sitting down again.

"No!" Jocelyn raised a hand in protest. "You will get nothing but lies from him. You know if he has lied to you all of your life, he is not suddenly going to do an about-face and be honest with you."

"You are right." His face took on a despairing expression. "But I must find out."

"Edward, do you think . . . is it possible . . ." She hesitated, dreading to express the thought.

"Is what possible?"

"Is it possible that, instead of being your brother, Sir Rolf could be your father?"

"God forbid!" The blood drained from Edward's face. "Having him for a brother has been trial enough. I could not stand to think . . . but yes, it is possible, I suppose."

Neither spoke for several minutes as they went over in their minds the enormity of this possibility.

After a while, Edward's eyes narrowed and he said, as though the question had just occurred to him, "Jocelyn, how did you come to go to the graves? Were you merely exploring and came across them, or was there a reason?"

"There was a reason," she interrupted. "Some days ago I was walking in the woods and came to the cottage of Maeve McCaulay, the seamstress. I stopped to talk with her for a while and during our conversation, she implied that all was not as it should be at Caradoc Court. She would not tell me anything outright, but she suggested that I go down the stairs beside the altar in the chapel and look at the graves. I forgot the whole conversation in the excitement of our other discoveries and remembered only this morning."

"What would Maeve know about the Caradoc family, or their graves?" Edward asked. "To my knowledge, she has never been inside the chapel, certainly not beneath it to the graves."

"Perhaps she saw them before the chapel was built over them," Jocelyn said.

"Yes, that could be. But again, what would she know

about the family? She has been living in the cottage in the woods for no more than a dozen or so years. I think she came from Ireland originally and worked in a tavern in the village. Rolf brought her here as seamstress when Mary, our old seamstress, died."

"I find her attitude both toward the Caradoc family and toward me quite strange," Jocelyn said. "At times I get the feeling that she is sorry for me—in some odd way, pities me—and at other times I get the feeling that she resents me, though I haven't any notion why she should."

"I think we should go to see Maeve and ask her, face to face, to explain what she knows about the date on my mother's . . . on Beatrice's gravestone."

"I doubt if she will tell us anything," Jocelyn said. "I tried to find out more from her when I was there, but she would say nothing else."

"Perhaps with me along to demand rather than just to ask nicely, she will say more," Edward said.

"All right," Jocelyn said, rising from the table. "If you think it will do any good, I am ready to try."

"Shall we walk through the woods or take the carriage and go by the highway?" Edward asked.

"Oh, a walk would be nice, it is such a lovely day."

"And what time do you have to be back to go in to Rolf?"

She laughed. "I have not been going to see him regularly since we found out . . ." she looked toward Hugo and finished ". . . what we found out. I did see him this morning and informed him that he need not expect me this afternoon."

"Good Lord! Did he take the roof off the house in rage?"

"No," she smiled, "your brother is becoming a bit milder in his tantrums. Mellowing, almost."

"I can't imagine it," Edward said. "How did you ac-complish that miracle?"

They both sobered, remembering that Rolf and Edward might not be brothers, but father and son; however, she continued speaking in a light vein. "There was no miracle involved. When I found out we were not married, I lost my fear of him. I simply told him I did not find it con-venient to go to his room twice a day for long periods. When he saw that he could not have his way merely by demanding it or going into a rage, he began to act with more civility. I think," she ended, "he has a disposition much like a spoiled child. He has been allowed to have his own way for too many years."

"After father died, there was never anyone to say no to him, to keep him from having or doing whatever he wanted," Edward said. "And even when father was living, I cannot remember a single instance of his correcting Rolf or telling him to do or not to do anything. I sup-pose by the time I came along, Rolf's ways were set."

As they walked out of the dining room, Edward took her hand. "Jocelyn, if he is my father . . . Rolf, that is . . . It is a terrible thought, but I must consider it. If he is my father, how much will that change your opinion of me?"

She wanted to say, "I love you, Edward, and nothing can change that love," but since he had not yet declared his love for her, she could not say it. Instead she answered, "Let us wait and see what we can find out from Maeve. We can cross bridges as we get to them, not before."

They walked through the woods holding hands like small children. Jocelyn thought of Hansel and Gretel on their way to the witch's gingerbread cottage, and she wanted to mention it to Edward, but when she looked at him, he appeared to be in such deep, intensely painful thought that she decided not to bother him. They went the whole way without either speaking a word.

When Maeve's cottage was in sight, Edward stopped and looked at it as though he were almost afraid to go on—afraid of what he might learn there.

"It is better to know," Jocelyn said softly, "than to spend a lifetime wondering."

Edward turned and gave her a slight smile. "How perceptive you are," he said. "That is exactly what I was thinking. As long as I have to know any of it, I think I should know all of it. But I cannot help wishing that . . . if it turns out that Rolf is my father . . . I cannot help wishing that I had never found out anything at all!"

Maeve was not sitting in front with her sewing today as she was the last time Jocelyn came. In fact, the place looked deserted. There was no sign of life and no sound from inside. Jocelyn's heart sank as she thought, What if she is not here? What if she has gone for good?

However, in answer to Edward's knock upon the door, they heard footsteps, and in a moment Maeve opened the door. There was no hiding the surprise on her face when she recognized her two visitors.

"Well, lookit!" she exclaimed. "What is it the two of you are doing here? Another accident in the forest?" She gave a shrill, nervous little laugh.

"No accident this time, Maeve," Edward said cheerfully, as Jocelyn bade the woman a good-afternoon. "We came to have a little talk with you."

"Now what would the two of you be wanting to talk to the likes of me about? Some sewing you want done, my lady?"

"No, Maeve," Jocelyn said. "I would like to continue the conversation we started the other day when I was here."

"Started and finished," Maeve said, "because I remember no conversation with you except about the weather and my inquiring as to the health of Sir Rolf."

Jocelyn saw that the woman was becoming more ill at ease—if not downright frightened—every minute. "You have nothing to worry about," she told her quickly. "We shall never let anyone know where our information came from."

Maeve's expression was one of assumed innocence as she said, "And what information might you be talking about? 'Tisn't likely that I have any information about anything, now is it?"

"Maeve," Edward said, his tone very serious, "let us not try to fool each other. You know . . ."

"La me! 'Tis you trying to make a fool of me, Mr. Edward. Sure and you know I never leave my house. What information could I have that you want?"

Jocelyn sat down on the bench in front of the cottage and then Edward did also, and motioned for Maeve to come out of the doorway and join them outside. The woman did, but hesitantly. She sat down on a barrel that had been made into a seat.

"Now then," Edward said. "Jocelyn did as you suggested, Maeve. She went to the graves under the chapel and by studying the dates on the stones, she found out that Beatrice was not my mother. That leaves the possibility that Sir Charles was not my father. You apparently knew this all the time, or you would not have suggested to Jocelyn that all was not as it should be at Caradoc Court. We are here to find out about my parentage and anything else you can tell us."

"You are talking gibberish," Maeve said. "You make no sense a-tall."

"We are going to sit here until you tell us, Maeve," Jocelyn said, adding as an afterthought, "and if it takes too long, Sir Rolf will send someone to look for us. He will wonder why we are spending so much time here."

"He knows you are here?" Maeve looked startled. "Sir Rolf knows?"

"Not yet," Edward said quickly, seeing an advantage and taking it, "but he will unless you tell us what we want to know."

Maeve emitted a long sigh and clasped her hands together in her lap. "I knew the minute I'd spoken to you that I had said too much," she said to Jocelyn. "I told myself then that I would live to regret ever opening my mouth to you."

"You will have nothing to regret if you tell us what we want to know," Jocelyn said.

"What is it you want to know?"

"Everything," Edward said promptly. "Start at the beginning."

Maeve gave each of them a pleading look, as though begging them not to make her reveal any part of what she knew, then she looked down at her lap as she clasped and unclasped her hands repeatedly. "Where to begin?" she said finally. "I can answer one of your questions." She looked at Edward. "Sir Charles was your father. There is no doubt about that."

"Thank God," Edward breathed, then added immediately, "but who was my mother?"

Maeve bowed her head so that both Edward and Jocelyn had to bend forward to hear her. "Lady Beatrice died . . . of the fever, I understand . . . and Sir Charles was beside himself with grief. Some months after her death, he went traveling to try to get over his hurt. Rolf was just seventeen then and Sir Charles left him at home to finish his education.

"Sir Charles went to Ireland and as he was getting over

his wife's death, he met and fell in love with a much younger girl named Ann Mary. He married her and for a few weeks they traveled about Ireland together, and then she became pregnant. Sir Charles wanted to bring his bride back here to Fenwick Manor—as the place was known then—but she was a fragile little thing and could not stand the trip to Buckinghamshire until after the baby was born. So Sir Charles remained in Ireland with her. Then you were born, Mr. Edward, and Ann Mary died giving birth. She was just too small, too fragile . . ." There were tears in Maeve's eyes now. "Like a tiny, easily broken toy, she was."

She was silent for several minutes, and Edward said, "So then my father brought me back here?"

"Yes," Maeve nodded. "Ann Mary was buried near the home where she had always lived, and Sir Charles brought you here with me to look after you. You may not know this because you were too young to remember, but I was your nursemaid until you were three."

"Why only until I was three?" Edward asked. "Did you not want to stay on? The nursemaid I remember was named Jenny."

"Oh, yes, I wanted to stay on, but . . ." She hesitated again. "It seemed best that someone else take over my duties. I went into the village to live."

"Why is it I never knew who my mother was?" Edward asked. "Do you know?"

Maeve shook her head. "I've not a notion, sir. I remember that Rolf was bitten raw with jealousy over his father's new son, and refused to have anything to do with you for as long as I was here. Later, I heard he treated you with only passing civility even after you were both grown up. I think maybe Sir Charles would have told you about your real mother—for he did love her with all his heart—after you were old enough to take it all in, but . . ."

"Yes," Edward interrupted, "I was still a small boy when he died. I am surprised, however, that Rolf never told me, surprised that he would let me go through life thinking we were full brothers when, in fact, we are only half brothers."

"He had his reasons, I am sure," Maeve said. "He has never done anything without a reason."

"He probably took some sort of perverted pleasure in letting me think that we had the same mother and that I was the cause of her death," Edward said bitterly. "That would be like Rolf." He looked at Jocelyn, "I told you he always tried to make me feel as though I were a murderer."

"He has never done anything without a reason," Maeve repeated.

"If only we could find out what some of those reasons are," Jocelyn said.

Maeve turned to Jocelyn as though she had forgotten she was there, as though her revelation, meant only for Edward, had been directed only to Edward—and now she thought of Jocelyn as an unwanted eavesdropper.

Her thick eyebrows knit together as a deep frown caused furrows across her weatherbeaten face. Her eyes shone with—what was it? . . . resentment? . . . hatred?—as she looked at the younger woman.

Jocelyn felt herself cringing under that look. If Edward were not here with her, she would actually be afraid of this strange, unfathomable woman who knew so many secrets.

"I never wanted to be the one to tell this," she said, "but while I am telling, I will tell you something else." Maeve's eyes, in tiny slits now, glinted as did a cat's as she continued to stare at Jocelyn.

"Your marriage to Sir Rolf, my pretty lady, is no marriage a-tall, because a man can only have one wife . . . and I am his wife."

Fifteen

Sir Rolf sat in his chair by the window, leaning forward in order to see the entire courtyard below. He had been in this position for so long that the old pain had returned to his back. Finally, he got up and walked slowly around the room, catching at a chair or the side of the bed when he seemed about to lose his balance.

The carriage had not left the house all day, so he knew Jocelyn and Edward were not riding. But he knew that, wherever they were, they were probably together.

Earlier, he had sent for Jocelyn's abigail, but he had learned nothing from her. Irva had looked like a scared rabbit when she had come into his room, bobbed a quick curtsy and said, "You wanted to see me, sir?" as though she was sure there must have been some mistake, or else John had not heard his orders correctly.

"Where is your mistress?" Sir Rolf asked, purposely making his tone of voice anything but gentle, thinking that if the girl were scared enough, she might tell him all he wanted to know.

"I do not know, sir. She did not return to the room after breakfast."

Ah! he thought, I have found out something already. "You mean she does not have her breakfast in her apartment? She goes to the dining room?"

Too late, Irva realized her mistake in giving out this involuntary information. "She went to the dining room this morning, sir. Usually, she has her meals in her room, except for the ones she has here with you."

"You know very well that she has not taken her meals here for some time." He glared at her. "Where is she now."

"I do not know, sir."

"When do you expect her to return to her rooms?"

"I do not know, sir."

"God's nightshirt! but you are a know-nothing!" If he had had anything in his hands then, or if any object had been close enough for him to get his hands on it, he would have thrown it at her. She was as aggravating as Jocelyn. "Get out of here!" he yelled. "No, wait! Go to the kitchen and tell Hugo I want to see him this instant. This *very* instant!"

Irva fled, and it was not long before Hugo appeared in the doorway.

"Well come in, come in. There is no need for you to stand there shifting from one foot to the other like an idiot!" Sir Rolf roared.

Hugo advanced a few steps into the room. "Yes, sir."

"I presume you served breakfast to my wife and my brother this morning."

"Yes, sir."

"Tell me about it."

"Yes, sir. I served them some porridge and . . ."

"You blithering idiot! I care not a damn what they ate! I want to know what they said to each other."

"I did not hear anything they said, sir. As soon as they were served, I went to the far side of the room, as I always do. As you told me always to do," he added.

Sir Rolf wanted to take a knife and cut the man's

throat as he would a deer he had just killed. But he knew he must try to remain calm or he would get no information whatever. "When they left the dining room, where did they go?"

"Uh—I am not sure, sir."

The man obviously knew more than he was telling. "Did they go to the gardens?"

"Uh—I believe not, sir."

It was all too much. He could stand no more of this —and from his own servant, at that. He stood up and walked over to Hugo. "If you value your life, you will tell me where they went." He said it in such a way that the man would know he meant what he said.

"I—I am not sure, sir," Hugo was looking at him as though wondering if he really would resort to murder. Obviously, the butler decided he would, for he added, "When they left the dining room, I believe they went outside."

"And where outside did they go?"

"As I was taking the dishes back to the kitchen, I chanced to see them, and . . . uh, I am not sure, but I think they may have been going toward the woods behind the house."

"You may go now, Hugo."

As soon as the butler had left the room, Sir Rolf kicked the bed post with all of his strength, and then howled with pain and limped quickly to the chair.

Sneaking off to the woods, were they? Like a low-class lackey and a tavern wench. Well, he would not put up with that sort of behavior from either of them. He would have Edward taken care of at once, and as for Jocelyn— if it was necessary to beat obedience into her, then he would do it with his cane.

He rested his head on the back of the chair and closed his eyes until the pain in his leg became less sharp. At the same time, his thinking seemed to become clearer.

He knew that neither Edward nor Jocelyn would deceive him by going into the woods together. Although it was quite evident that neither liked him, he knew that they both made much of honor, and that they would not dishonor themselves in that common fashion.

Why, then, were they going into the woods together?

He could think of one reason and one reason only: Maeve.

The thought made him break out in cold perspiration. His hands began to tremble as a sick feeling engulfed him.

Then, another thought made him feel better: surely Maeve would have enough sense to keep her mouth shut. Surely she realized that if she told more than she should, he would have unspeakable things done to her.

He had been afraid that she would say more than she should to Jocelyn on that night of the accident when they had spent the night in her cottage. Therefore, he had kept Maeve with him until Jocelyn had gone to bed —after, of course, ascertaining that Maeve had told Jocelyn nothing on their way back to where he lay suffering on the ground. By morning, he was sure that Maeve would say nothing. The woman was not an idiot; she obviously knew her future depended upon her silence.

Just as his future did. Finally, after years of waiting, he had everything he had always wanted—or he would have very soon now—as soon as he was able to leave this room and take his rightful place in the household and as Jocelyn's husband. He had gone to considerable lengths and much trouble to arrange everything just as he wanted it. If Maeve talked, all of his plans would blow away like so much smoke on a windy day.

But Maeve would say nothing; he knew he could count on her. He always had.

He pulled the bell-cord and when John appeared, he

said, "Tell my wife and my brother I wish to see them as soon as they return."

He would put a stop, once and for all time, to their walks, their rides, and their cozy meals taken together in the dining room. Somehow, he would think of a way before they returned to make sure they never saw each other again.

At the cottage in the woods, the silence after Maeve's statement was like the silence after a deafening clap of thunder. There was no sound whatever, not even a bird call, yet not one of the three people in front of the cottage noticed the stillness, so engrossed were they in their thoughts.

It was Edward who finally broke the spell with the words, "What did you say?" He could not believe what he had heard, or what he thought he had heard.

"I said Sir Rolf could not be married to this fine lady because he is married to me," Maeve said. "Oh yes, Mr. Edward, it is quite a legal marriage. You can look in the Book of Records at the county seat if you do not believe me."

Jocelyn, in a daze, was shaking her head. "It cannot be."

"Just have a look in the Book of Records," Maeve said. "You will find my name and . . ." She broke off a moment, then said, "Sir Rolf used his two middle names, John Warren, with the Caradoc so no one would know at the time, but it is still quite legal. I made sure of that."

"When were you married?" Edward asked.

"Twelve years ago," Maeve said. "In April of 1802. April the eighth, to be exact."

"How—how did you come to marry Rolf?" Edward asked.

"You think it impossible that he would want to marry

me, do you?" Maeve asked. "I'll have you know I was a fair-looking girl in my day and . . ."

"Please tell us, Maeve, how it all came about," Edward said.

Jocelyn, still not knowing what to think of this completely unexpected turn of events, fastened her eyes upon this woman who claimed to be Sir Rolf's legal wife of twelve years, and listened intently as Maeve began another explanation of the past.

She laughed. "Quite a good-looking girl, I was, when I first came here from Ireland. Sir Rolf was always around with some foolishness from the very beginning. Just could not keep his hands off me, he couldn't. That is why I left here when you were only three." She looked at Edward. "Sir Charles thought it best to have me off the place, out of reach of Rolf, so to speak. So Sir Charles got them to take me on in the village as a tavern maid."

She laughed again. "It didn't take Rolf long to find me, however. Within the year he had come to the tavern and spotted me. And one night, not long after that, he came to the tavern and said he wanted to have a private talk with me, that there were things I should know. So we went to my little room over the tavern, and before I knew what was what, he had his way with me, and . . ."

"You can spare us the details," Edward said quickly, looking at Jocelyn.

Maeve nodded and continued, "I became his fancy-piece after that. He came to the tavern right often, he did. Oh, but we had some high old times, the two of us. No one in the whole countryside could have had better. Drinking our ale and laughing at anything and everything. And one night, after we had both had a bit too much of liquid high spirits, Rolf says to me, 'Maeve, m'girl, I will wager a goodly amount that if I asked you, you would be willing to marry me.' And I told him he would win that wager from anyone foolish enough to bet against him. So he said, 'All right then, we can go wake up the magistrate right now, make it all legal and proper, and I can show everybody that Sir Rolf Caradoc can get married any time he wants to.' "

She paused and looked from one to the other of them as though expecting some comment, but none was forthcoming so she continued. "Rolf was a bit soberer by the time we got the magistrate up, but he still wanted to go through with the marriage, even though he signed the book John Warren Caradoc instead of Rolf John Warren Caradoc. I think he thought it would be a good joke on the whole world: Sir Rolf Caradoc marrying a tavern maid." Maeve laughed uproariously now, as though it was a joke she still enjoyed.

"By the next morning he was not quite so amused," she said, her expression becoming glum now. "Got a bit nasty, he did, and told me he wanted to keep the scandalous affair quiet and his tavern wench wife out of sight. I told him he'd best treat me right or I would raise quite a ruckus, and he told me it would not be healthy for me if I did. Purely threatened me, he did. I told him I was not going to be a tavern maid any longer, because it was not a fitting position for his wife. That was when he brought me to this cottage in the woods to keep me out of sight, and told everyone that I was the new seamstress. Couldn't even sew at the time." She laughed bitterly now. "But I learned."

She gave a deep sigh. "After he brought me here, he just left me. Left me completely alone, he did. I didn't see him from one year to the next, but I heard plenty about how he was having his way with every housemaid and tavern wench in the county, and how no proper lady would receive him. Made me laugh, it did, and I said good enough for him!"

"And you never said anything to anybody about it in all these years?" To Jocelyn this was the most amazing aspect of the story she had just heard: that Maeve had told no one she was the wife of Sir Rolf Caradoc. Obviously Maeve had no feeling for the man now, but surely she must have at one time.

"Never told a living soul," Maeve said. "Not a soul. And I wouldn't have mentioned it now except . . . I would have gone to my grave with the secret if Sir Rolf had acted decently, if he had done the decent thing by me."

"You did not consider that he had done the decent thing by you when he married you?" Edward asked.

"I mean after he married me," Maeve said. "I mean when he was planning to marry this fine and proper lady here. If he had come to me and said what he was about to do and asked me to continue to hold my peace, I would have. If he had acted like a decent human being instead of always thinking he was the High Lord Almighty who could do no wrong . . ." She stopped and looked at the ground, obviously moved almost to tears for the first time in her long recital.

"I would have kept the secret forever," she said after a few minutes. "I did not know one thing about his marriage . . ." She spat out the word with contempt—"until the night after that so-called wedding when his bride," now she gave Jocelyn a hard look, "tried to run away from him, and he followed her into the woods and fell off his horse. That was good enough for him too! Never could ride worth a tinker's! I wouldn't have cared if his back had been broken."

Jocelyn nodded, understanding the woman's attitude entirely. Had she been in Maeve's place, she would not have cared either had Sir Rolf suffered serious injury.

"I was so furious with him," Maeve went on, "that I

decided that very night that I would tell everything, and I would do it at the time I thought it would do the most good . . . or harm to him. I never meant any harm to you, though, Mr. Edward. I want you to believe that. But I could not think of another way to get this lady to come back to see me unless I got her curious about the dates on those stones. Even then, I did not think she would come back, because I did not think she would know enough about the family to notice that the dates were not just right."

"I understand now," Jocelyn said. "I understand many things that I did not understand before."

"That last time you were here, missy," Maeve said to Jocelyn, "I had taken a spell of hating Sir Rolf for treating me the way he did and I decided it was time to start things a-rolling, and the main thing I wanted to see a-rolling was Sir Rolf's head! Anyway, I told you to look down the stairway beside the chapel. But I made a mistake in sizing you up. I thought you would go a-running to Sir Rolf with your questions and embarrass him and force the truth out of him. Instead, you went to Mr. Edward and then came to me. I hadn't figured on that."

"I would never have thought of connecting you with the discrepancy in the dates," Jocelyn said. "I would never have known the part you have played in Sir Rolf's life, for had I gone straight to him, he would have made up something to tell me. I am sure I would never have gotten the true story from him."

"Like as not he would have lied," Maeve agreed. "Telling the truth is not one of his strong points."

Edward, who had been staring into the forest in deep concentration, now brought his attention back to the two women. "I am wondering," he said slowly, "what to do with the truth now that we know it."

"Do whatever will knock His Lordship off his high horse," Maeve said, and then cackled, "B'gorra, you knocked him off once, missy, and I would like to see you do it again, I would."

Jocelyn gave her a weak smile. She was not quite sure how to take Maeve or what the woman's attitude toward her was. One minute Maeve seemed to resent her, and the next minute it was as though they were good friends and strong allies. Then she looked at Edward, begging him with her eyes to make the move to go. She did not want to stay here any longer. There was no need to stay; they had learned all they could from Maeve, and now she wanted to get away by herself to sort things out in her mind. Right now, she felt as though she would spend the rest of her life trying to get rid of the past weeks' accumulation of confusion in her mind, all of which had culminated in the knowledge of Sir Rolf's nefarious scheming.

Edward, seeing and understanding her look, stood up. "Thank you, Maeve," he said. "I will see that you never have reason to regret telling us the facts of my birth . . . and of your marriage."

"Oh, I won't be regretting it," Maeve said stoutly. "If His Lordship ever tries to throw me out or decides he no longer wants to take care of me, all I have to do is threaten to spread the word around that I am Lady Maeve Caradoc. Ha! Now ain't that a good one? I have been laughing about that for twelve years, I have."

"I thank you also," Jocelyn said. "It was good of you . . ."

"I didn't tell you anything to be good," Maeve interrupted. "And I didn't tell you *for* anyone's good."

"Nevertheless," Jocelyn said, "I think the truth will be good for everyone, except possibly Sir Rolf. And even he should feel some relief at not having to go on living a lie."

"Not Rolf, I'm afraid," Edward said. "After a lifetime spent in lying, I doubt that he can now separate his lies from the truth."

Thanking Maeve again, they left, picking their way back down the narrow path through the woods.

"It will take me a while to be able to grasp all of this," Jocelyn said. "It seems to be too much to take in all at once."

"I know," Edward agreed, taking her arm to keep her from stumbling along the path. "All my life I have thought Beatrice Caradoc was my mother, and now I find out she was not, and that my mother was a woman I never heard of." He shook his head. "And Rolf is not my full brother, but my half brother. That, at least, is not bad news."

"When you stop to think about it, is any of it really bad news?" Jocelyn asked.

"No," Edward said. "I never knew anything about Beatrice except what I was told, so there is no pain in finding out that she was not my mother. And I actually feel better knowing Rolf is only a half-brother. The less relation I am to him, the better I like it. And as for finding out that he is married to Maeve . . ." He broke off and began laughing.

"What do you find so amusing about that?" she asked.

"The fact that Rolf went to such extremes to keep the marriage a secret when actually I think it was Maeve who married beneath her."

Jocelyn laughed with him. "I think you are right."

"Everything is clear now," Edward said. "We know why Rolf did not get the vicar to perform your ceremony, but hired an impostor instead. Had it been a real ceremony and the truth about Maeve came out, he could be sent to gaol for bigamy."

"He staged the marriage so he could appear to be married to me," she said.

"Yes, he thought no one would ever be the wiser and he could have an heir by a proper lady. Strange that he never considered the fact that his 'proper heir' would be illegitimate." Edward seemed to find this amusing also, but Jocelyn did not.

She changed the subject. "It seems to me we have to let Sir Rolf know that we know everything. And . . . and I think I must go back to Egmont House now. It is unseemly and improper that I stay on at Caradoc Court."

Edward stopped and looked at her. "Go home? Leave now—now that everything has turned out just right for us? I thought—have you no feeling at all for me? Have I been misinterpreting everything you have said and done these past few days? Have I misread every gesture, every look?"

Jocelyn, embarrassed, could not meet his eyes. Had she been behaving so brazenly? Had she been declaring her love for him in endless ways so openly when he had not once made any kind of declaration to her other than to say that one time, "You are my love"?

"I thought . . . I was sure that you cared for me," Edward said. "At least a little. I thought I had come to know you well enough to guess, almost, what you were thinking."

"Perhaps you have come to know me too well, sir," she said, quite formally, adding coldly, "under the circumstances."

"What circumstances?" Edward looked truly perplexed. "I am beginning to think that I do not know you at all. Now, when we should be closer than we have ever been, you have suddenly become a stranger."

"I have always thought," she said airily, "that it was proper for a gentleman to express his own feelings before demanding to know those of a lady."

"But Jocelyn, I thought you knew how I felt! I have told you outright and in a hundred other different ways. How could you doubt?"

"But you have actually said nothing," she protested, "nothing to make me think you were serious. Not even after we found out that Sir Rolf and I were not man and wife."

"I deliberately restrained myself from asking you to marry me then," he said. "I was afraid, if you agreed, that we might later uncover some terrible family secret that would make you change your mind. I could not have borne that. I wanted to wait until we found out the reason for Rolf's strange actions." He stopped her on the path and turned to face her. "And now that we know, I feel free to speak. What is it you wish, Miss Egmont? A proper proposal of marriage? Shall I get down on my knees to you right here in the forest?"

"No, no," she laughed, tugging at his arm as he started to go down on one knee. "All I want . . . all I have ever wanted was to hear you say . . ."

"I love you, Jocelyn. I have loved you from the first moment I saw you even though I did not realize at the time that it was love."

He bent and kissed her and she felt for the first time in months that all was right again with the world . . . her world.

"What would your answer have been, had I made a proper proposal?" he asked, a twinkle in his eyes.

"It would have been yes, of course."

"Good! Now we can begin to make plans." The smile on his face faded as he added, "But first we have an unpleasant task to perform. It is time for us to confront Rolf now."

"And Gerard!" she exclaimed. "I had completely forgotten about Gerard!"

Sixteen

When they reached the house, they went immediately to Sir Rolf's room and found him walking about on unsteady legs. He looked at them with distrust plainly showing in his face.

"Damme! you are bold, the two of you!" were his first words. "You have the unmitigated gall to come in here together after I have expressly told you both you are to have nothing to do with each other."

"And the doctor told you you were to stay off your feet for at least a month," Edward said lightly. "It seems no one takes orders very seriously any more."

Sir Rolf gave him a quizzical look. "I am a better judge of my health and my capabilities than anyone else," he said. "And I am a better judge of what is best for my wife. Edward, if you do not stay away from Jocelyn, I shall have you horsewhipped! God's nightshirt, man! Have you no sense of honor whatever?"

"See who is talking about a sense of honor!" Jocelyn said in amazement, and that remark caused Sir Rolf to give her a long, scrutinizing look. He evidently decided at that point that this was no casual, social visit. He hobbled to the window and sank down in his chair. "I am tired," he said. "I may have been overdoing it a trifle, and I need my rest now."

"You shall have it," Edward said, "as soon as we have said what we came to say. Then you can rest for the rest of your life."

Jocelyn had thought she would enjoy this scene, watching Sir Rolf squirm and admit to wrongdoing, so she was unprepared for the sudden feeling of pity that came over her. The man looked so uncomfortable, so ill-at-ease, that his efforts to keep a bland expression on his face were in vain. Perhaps, she thought, he half expects what is coming. And then she thought, It must be a terrible thing to see all of your plans, a lifetime of hope, turn to naught. She could not help feeling a little sorry for him, remembering how she had felt when Gerard had told her she must give up her lifetime of hopes by marrying this man. To give up your hopes and dreams is to give up your life, she thought. That is what I did, and that is what he will do now.

Sir Rolf looked from one to the other of them in somewhat anguished expectation. Jocelyn waited for Edward to speak first, wondering which of Sir Rolf's many sins of omission and commission he would bring up first. She did not have to wait long.

"Rolf, why did you never tell me that you and I did not have the same mother?"

A look of relief spread instantly over Sir Rolf's face, as though he were saying to himself, Is this all they came about?

"Never seemed important," he said, adding in a heartier voice, "always thought of you as a full brother."

Edward let that remark pass, but he could not resist saying, "Just as you always thought of Jocelyn as your real wife?"

Both Edward and Jocelyn saw the blood drain from Sir Rolf's face, leaving him with a deathlike pallor. "What do you mean?" he said, scarcely above a whisper. "What are you saying?"

"I am saying that Jocelyn and I know everything now, about your wife, Maeve, whom you have kept hidden in the forest all these years, about how you hired the innkeeper, Thaddeus Jonas, to pose as a vicar and officiate at a sham ceremony, about your plans to live with Jocelyn, letting her think she was actually married to you, so you could have an heir . . ."

"Stop!" Sir Rolf cried, holding up his hand, and when Edward stopped, the silence that fell over the room was far more expressive than any words could have been. It was obvious that Sir Rolf knew his defeat was total and that there would be no point in trying to deny any of the charges Edward had made against him.

"How . . . how did you find out . . . all of it?" he asked finally.

Jocelyn shook her head at Edward, meaning for him to say nothing about Maeve's revelations. That poor woman's life was lonely enough without their making things worse for her.

"I found out about the discrepancy in the dates between Edward's birth and Lady Beatrice's death," she said quickly. "And I recognized the innkeeper at The Cloak and Candle as the vicar who performed the marriage ceremony."

"And I went into the county seat straightaway and saw that no marriage between you and Jocelyn had been recorded," Edward said.

"You found out about Maeve by looking in the Book of Records also?" Sir Rolf asked weakly.

"You were registered as John Warren Caradoc, were you not?" Edward said. "You did not use your full name."

Lovely! Jocelyn thought. Edward had managed not to implicate Maeve, and still he had not lied himself.

"Of course I did not use my full name!" Sir Rolf's voice was coming back. He was roaring now. "Do you think I wanted the whole world to know I married a tavern wench while I was in a drunken haze?" He calmed down somewhat and looked at Edward. "What are you going to do?"

Jocelyn looked away. There was no enjoyment whatever in seeing the suffering of this man she had so detested. His agony of wondering what would be exacted of him in retribution for his misdeeds showed plainly in his face. If she had ever wanted to see him as miserable as he had made her these past weeks, the thought completely left her mind now.

"We are not going to do anything that you need worry about," she said, and the words seemed to take Edward by surprise for he turned and looked at her. Then, apparently understanding and agreeing with her reasoning, he nodded and said, "I am taking Jocelyn and her abigail back to Egmont House as soon as they are packed and ready to go, and there we will make preparations for a real wedding."

"You?" Sir Rolf asked.

"Yes, Jocelyn and I are going to be married as soon as the necessary arrangements can be made," Edward said, looking at Jocelyn to be sure she agreed to these up-to-now undiscussed plans.

She smiled. "I am sure we have your best wishes, Sir Rolf."

"My wish is that I had never laid eyes upon you—either of you!" And with that he turned his back upon them and stared moodily out the window.

That was the way they left him.

The ride from Caradoc Court to Egmont House was the exact opposite, in more ways than direction, of the ride from Egmont House to Caradoc Court. Jocelyn felt that she was grinning like a ninny the entire journey. She and Irva and Edward talked very little, each seemingly lost in contented daydreams. As they neared their destination, Irva spoke.

"What is Mr. Gerard going to say about our coming home?"

Although the question was addressed to Jocelyn, it was Edward who answered. "He had better be careful what he says about anything. I am not feeling too kindly disposed toward Jocelyn's brother—any more than she is toward mine," he added with a laugh.

It was not long before they found out what Gerard would say. He was standing in front of Egmont House when the carriage came through the gates. He had been in his room upstairs and had recognized the carriage as soon as it turned from the road.

Gerard's pallor matched that of Sir Rolf as he watched Edward help Jocelyn and Irva out. He approached them slowly, an expression of dread on his face. "Where is Sir Rolf? I trust this is merely a visit?"

"That is hardly a proper greeting, is it, Gerard? After all, you have not seen me since my wedding day," Jocelyn said cheerfully.

"Where is Sir Rolf?" he repeated. "Why did he not come with you?"

"We left him in rather poor health and low spirits," Edward said. "It will be a while before he can travel any distance, or *want* to travel any distance, for that matter."

Gerard continued to stare at them as though not certain whether they were real or figments of his imagination. When Edward began to take portmanteaux from the carriage, Gerard appeared to be on the verge of a fainting spell.

"Do you suppose you could get someone to help me

with these?" Edward asked. "I do not think I can manage the trunk by myself."

"What . . . what . . ." Gerard could not get the words out.

"I have come home, dear brother," Jocelyn said, enjoying this scene much more than the one with Sir Rolf. "Are you not glad to see me?"

"I was planning to go to Caradoc Court tomorrow to see Sir Rolf . . . and you, of course," Gerard said. He was still looking from one to the other as though he wanted an explanation but was afraid to ask for one. "Come inside," he said finally, "and tell me why you are here—and your husband is not."

Irva went to the back of the house to find someone to take the trunk and portmanteaux upstairs while Jocelyn, Edward, and Gerard went to the large, closed parlor.

"Mercy, Gerard!" Jocelyn exclaimed as she went from window to window opening the shutters. "I do not think this room has been aired out since I was here."

"I should not be surprised," Gerard said. "I have been away a good deal of the time."

"London?" Edward asked, "or the continent?"

"Both."

"I am not surprised," Jocelyn said.

"Are you going to tell me?" Gerard said.

"I would like to tell you a few things," Edward said, "but not in your sister's presence. Any man who . . ." He broke off, not trusting himself to go on.

"It seems, Gerard, that your carefully planned future for me did not work out exactly as you thought it would," Jocelyn said.

Gerard, already pale, grew paler. "What are you talking about?"

They told him, first Jocelyn, then Edward chiming in with more details, about Sir Rolf's marriage to Maeve, the staged wedding ceremony with the innkeeper as vicar, and of the plans to keep Jocelyn at Caradoc Court as wife to Sir Rolf. They did not tell him about Rolf's deception to Edward about his mother as neither could see any reason for Gerard to know.

When they finished, Gerard seemed to be going from a highly nervous state into a fine frenzy. "But this cannot be true, it cannot be true!" he said over and over.

"Why were you planning to go to Caradoc Court tomorrow, Gerard?" Jocelyn asked, remembering her brother's earlier statement.

Gerard slumped in his chair. "I suppose it makes no difference now if you know," he said. "The checks I have received from Sir Rolf have not been enough to . . . to cover my expenses. I was going to ask him to increase the amount."

"What you mean is that you have gambled everything away, is it not?" Edward asked.

Gerard looked down at the rug and said nothing.

"Of course, that is it," Jocelyn answered for him. "Well, Gerard, how much trouble are you in now."

"I heard yesterday that my debtors have gone to the magistrate and that I am likely to be thrown into debtors' gaol unless I can get the money I owe immediately," he said. "I was sure Sir Rolf would not give me enough, but I thought he would at least give me enough to get out of the country. I did not think he would want to see his brother-in-law in gaol."

"Nor would I," Edward said.

Gerard looked first at Edward, then at Jocelyn, and then, finally comprehending Edward's meaning, a smile began to play over his face. To Edward he said, "You and Jocelyn . . ."

"We plan to be married as soon as it can be arranged," Edward said.

"You will lend me the money then? To pay off those vultures?" Gerard wasted no time in his request.

Edward sighed. "I think . . ."

"If you are afraid I shall be after you constantly for money, you need not worry on that score," Gerard said. "As I said, I am leaving the country just as soon as I can get enough . . ."

"Where will you go?" Jocelyn asked.

"The continent. France first, maybe Switzerland . . . I am not sure . . ."

"Yes," Edward said. "I will let you have the money."

A huge sigh of relief escaped Gerard.

"On second thought," Edward said, "I will not let you have the money after all."

Gerard sat up on the edge of his chair. "But you promised. You said . . ."

"I think you should get the money from Rolf," Edward continued.

"But you know he will never let me have it. Not now!" Gerard wailed.

"Oh, I think your chances are better now than they ever were," Edward said, unperturbed by Gerard's growing agitation. "Just go to see Rolf and tell him you want retribution for all the mental stress he has put you through because of what he did to your sister. In order to keep you from telling the whole countryside, I am sure he will part with enough of his worldly possessions to keep you occupied in the gaming houses on the continent for a long time."

"But that is blackmail!" Gerard cried.

"I do believe it is," Edward said agreeably. "Heavens! That I would think you would stoop to blackmail."

Gerard sprang from his chair.

"Where are you going?" Jocelyn asked.

"To pack. I am leaving—for good—first thing in the morning."

"For the continent?" Edward asked.

"Yes—after a stop at Caradoc Court." He tore out of the room as though in a frightful hurry. Jocelyn and Edward both burst into uncontrollable laughter until they were weak.

"That takes care of our second problem—Rolf was the first one," Edward said finally. "But there is something else now, of a more serious nature, that we must decide."

"What is that?" Jocelyn asked.

"Where we are going to live after we are married. I know you do not want to go back to Caradoc Court. Nor do I."

Jocelyn stood up suddenly. "Come with me," she said. "I have something to show you."

She led the way outside, beyond the dark green hedges, to the rose garden where a few late-blooming roses still gave color to the garden. "You see," she said triumphantly, "it is very much like your own garden."

"Yes, it is," he said. "I do not wonder that my garden made you homesick."

"Do you think you could feel at home here . . . at Egmont House?" she asked.

He nodded. "From what I have seen of it, it is a lovely, comfortable place."

"Gerard will not be coming back," she said. "There is no reason why we could not live here . . . happily."

"No reason at all." He kissed her, then suddenly he looked at her and began laughing.

"What do you find so amusing?" she asked, feeling a little hurt by his laughter.

"I was thinking about Rolf," he said. "When Gerard appears tomorrow and demands—and gets—more money from him."

Jocelyn smiled.

"There is another even better joke on him," Edward
continued, his laughter increasing. "Since this is to be our
home, Rolf will have the entire care of Caradoc Court and
all the land. Since he has no aptitude—not to mention
liking—for that sort of thing, he will have enough work
to keep him out of trouble for the rest of his life."

"A fitting punishment for one who has never done any
work," Jocelyn said.

Edward stooped and picked a pink rosebud, carefully
took the thorns off, and gave it to Jocelyn. Then, arms
entwined, they went back into the house.

Historical Romance

☐ THE ADMIRAL'S LADY—Gibbs	P2658	1.25
☐ AFTER THE STORM—Williams	23081-3	1.50
☐ AN AFFAIR OF THE HEART—Smith	23092-9	1.50
☐ AS THE SPARKS FLY—Eastvale	P2569	1.25
☐ A BANBURY TALE—MacKeever	23174-7	1.50
☐ CLARISSA—Arnett	22893-2	1.50
☐ DEVIL'S BRIDE—Edwards	23176-3	1.50
☐ A FAMILY AFFAIR—Mellows	22967-X	1.50
☐ FIRE OPALS—Danton	23112-7	1.50
☐ THE FORTUNATE MARRIAGE—Trevor	23137-2	1.50
☐ FRIENDS AT KNOLL HOUSE—Mellows	P2530	1.25
☐ THE GLASS PALACE—Gibbs	23063-5	1.50
☐ GRANBOROUGH'S FILLY—Blanshard	23210-7	1.50
☐ HARRIET—Mellows	23209-3	1.50
☐ HORATIA—Gibbs	23175-5	1.50
☐ LEONORA—Fellows	22897-5	1.50
☐ LORD FAIRCHILD'S DAUGHTER— MacKeever	P2695	1.25
☐ MARRIAGE ALLIANCE—Stables	23142-9	1.50
☐ MELINDA—Arnett	P2547	1.25
☐ THE PHANTOM GARDEN—Bishop	23113-5	1.50
☐ THE PRICE OF VENGEANCE— Michel	23211-5	1.50
☐ THE RADIANT DOVE—Jones	P2753	1.25
☐ THE ROMANTIC FRENCHMAN—Gibbs	P2869	1.25
☐ SPRING GAMBIT—Williams	23025-2	1.50

Buy them at your local bookstore or use this handy coupon for ordering:

Sylvia Thorpe

Sparkling novels of love and conquest set against the colorful background of historic England. Here are stories you will savor word by word, page by spellbinding page into the wee hours of the night.

☐ BEGGAR ON HORSEBACK	23091-0	1.50
☐ CAPTAIN GALLANT	Q2709	1.50
☐ FAIR SHINE THE DAY	23229-8	1.75
☐ THE GOLDEN PANTHER	23006-6	1.50
☐ THE RELUCTANT ADVENTURESS	P2578	1.25
☐ ROGUE'S COVENANT	23041-4	1.50
☐ ROMANTIC LADY	Q2910	1.50
☐ THE SCANDALOUS LADY ROBIN	Q2934	1.50
☐ THE SCAPEGRACE	P2663	1.25
☐ THE SCARLET DOMINO	23220-4	1.50
☐ THE SILVER NIGHTINGALE	P2626	1.25
☐ THE SWORD AND THE SHADOW	22945-9	1.50
☐ SWORD OF VENGEANCE	23136-4	1.50
☐ TARRINGTON CHASE	Q2843	1.50